Also by Erle Stanley Gardner
Published by Ballantine Books:

The Case of the
Howling Dog

Erle Stanley Gardner

BALLANTINE BOOKS • NEW YORK

ISBN 0-345-31679-7

This edition published by arrangement with Severn House Publishers Ltd.

Manufactured in the United States of America

First Ballantine Books Edition: October 1984

Cast of Characters

IN THE ORDER OF THEIR APPEARANCE

CHAPTER I

Della Street held open the door to the inner office, and spoke in the tone which a woman instinctively uses in speaking to a child or a very sick man.

"Go right in, Mr. Cartright," she said. "Mr. Mason will see you."

A broad-shouldered, rather heavy-set man, of about thirty-two, with haunted brown eyes, walked into the office, and stared at the sober countenance of Perry Mason.

"You're Perry Mason," he asked, "the lawyer?"

Mason nodded.

"Sit down," he said.

The man dropped into the chair Mason had indicated with a gesture, mechanically reached for a package of cigarettes, took one out, conveyed it to his lips, and had the package half way back to his pocket before he thought to offer one to Perry Mason.

The hand that held the extended package of cigarettes trembled, and the lawyer's knowing eyes stared for a moment at the quivering hand before he shook his head.

"No," he said, "thank you, I've got my own brand."

The man nodded, hurriedly put the package of cigarettes back in his pocket, struck a match, and casually leaned forward, so that his elbow was resting on the arm of the chair, steadying the hand which held the match as he lit the cigarette.

"My secretary," said Perry Mason, in a calm tone of voice, "told me that you wanted to see me about a dog and about a will."

The man nodded. "A dog and a will," he repeated mechanically.

"Well," said Perry Mason, "let's talk about the will first. I don't know much about dogs."

Cartright nodded. His hungry brown eyes were fastened

1

upon Perry Mason with the expression of a very sick man looking at a competent physician.

Perry Mason took a pad of yellow foolscap from a drawer in his desk, picked up a desk pen, and said: "What's your name?"

"Arthur Cartright."

"Age?"

"Thirty-two."

"Residence?"

"4893 Milpas Drive."

"Married or single?"

"Do we need to go into that?"

Perry Mason held the pen poised above the foolscap while he raised his eyes to regard Cartright with steady appraisal.

"Yes," he said.

Cartright held the cigarette over an ashtray, and tapped the ashes from the end with a hand that shook as though with the ague.

"I don't think it makes any difference in the kind of a will I'm drawing up," he said.

"I've got to know," Perry Mason told him.

"But I tell you it won't make any difference, on account of the way I'm leaving my property."

Perry Mason said nothing, but the calm insistence of his very silence drove the other to speech.

"Yes," he said.

"Wife's name?"

"Paula Cartright, age twenty-seven."

"Residing with you?" asked Mason.

"No."

"Where does she reside?"

"I don't know," said the man.

Perry Mason hesitated a moment, and his quiet, patient eyes surveyed the haggard countenance of his client. Then he spoke soothingly.

"Very well," he said, "let's find out a little more about

what you want to do with your property before we go back to that. Have you any children?"

"No."

"How did you want to leave your property?"

"Before we go into that," said Cartright, speaking rapidly, "I want to know if a will is valid no matter how a man dies."

Perry Mason nodded his head, wordlessly.

"Suppose," said Cartright, "a man dies on the gallows or in the electric chair? You know, suppose he's executed for murder, then what happens to his will?"

"It makes no difference how a man dies, his will is not affected," Mason said.

"How many witnesses do I need to a will?"

"Two witnesses under certain circumstances," Mason said, "and none under others."

"How do you mean?"

"I mean that if a will is drawn up in typewriting, and you sign it, there must be two witnesses to your signature, but in this state, if a will is written entirely in your handwriting, including date and signature, and there is no other writing or printing on the sheet of paper, save your own handwriting, it does not need to have any witnesses to the signature. Such a will is valid and binding."

Arthur Cartright sighed, and his sigh seemed to be one of relief. When he spoke, his voice was more quiet, less jerky.

"Well," he said, "that seems to clear that point up."

"To whom did you want your property to go?" asked Perry Mason.

"To Mrs. Clinton Foley, living at 4889 Milpas Drive."

Perry Mason raised his eyebrows.

"A neighbor?" he asked.

"A neighbor," said Cartright, in the tone of voice of one who wishes to discourage comment.

"Very well," said Perry Mason, and then added: "Remember, Cartright, you're talking to a lawyer. Don't have secrets from your lawyer. Tell me the truth. I won't betray your confidences."

"Well," Cartright said impatiently, "I'm telling you everything, ain't I?"

Perry Mason's eyes and voice were both serene.

"I don't know," he said. "This was something that I was telling you. Now go ahead and tell me about your will."

"That's all of it."

"What do you mean?"

"I mean just that. The property all goes to Mrs. Clinton Foley; every bit of it."

Perry Mason put the pen back in its receptacle, and the fingers of his right hand made little drumming noises on the top of the desk. A wary appraisal was evident in his glance.

"Well, then," he said, "let's hear about the dog."

"The dog howls," said Cartright.

Perry Mason's nod was sympathetic.

"He howls mostly at night," Cartright said, "but sometimes during the day. It's driving me crazy. I can't stand that continual howling. You know, a dog howls when there's a death due to occur in the neighborhood."

"Where is the dog?" asked Mason.

"In the house next door."

"You mean," asked Perry Mason, "that the house where Mrs. Clinton Foley lives is on one side of you, and the house that has the howling dog is on the other side?"

"No," said Cartright, "I mean that the howling dog is in Clinton Foley's house."

"I see," Mason remarked. "Suppose you tell me *all* about it, Cartright."

Cartright pinched out the end of the cigarette, got to his feet, walked rapidly to the window, stared out with unseeing eyes, then turned and paced back toward the lawyer.

"Look here," he said, "there's one more question about the will."

"Yes?" asked Mason.

"Suppose Mrs. Clinton Foley really shouldn't be Mrs. Clinton Foley?"

"How do you mean?" Mason inquired.

"Suppose that she's living with Clinton Foley, as his wife, but isn't married to him?"

"That wouldn't make any difference," Mason said slowly, *"if* you described her in the will as 'Mrs. Clinton Foley, the woman who is at present living with Clinton Foley at 4889 Milpas Drive, as his wife.' In other words, the testator has a right to leave property to whom he wishes. Words of description in a will are valuable only so far as they explain the intention of the testator.

"For instance, there have been many occasions when men have died, willing property to their wives, and it has turned out they were not legally married. There have been cases where men have left property to their sons, when it has turned out that the person was not really his son. . . ."

"I don't care anything about all that stuff," said Arthur Cartright irritably. "I'm just asking you about this one particular case. It wouldn't make any difference?"

"It wouldn't make any difference," Mason said.

"Well, then," said Cartright, his eyes suddenly cunning. "Suppose that there should be a *real* Mrs. Clinton Foley. What I mean is, suppose Clinton Foley had been legally married and had never been legally divorced, and I should leave the property to Mrs. Clinton Foley?"

Perry Mason's tone of voice was that of one soothing groundless fears.

"I have explained to you," he said, "that the intention of the testator governs. If you leave your property to the woman who is *now* residing at that address, as the wife of Clinton Foley, it is all that is necessary. But do I understand that Clinton Foley is living?"

"Of course he's living. He's living next door to me."

"I see," Mason said cautiously, feeling his way, and making his voice sound casual. "And Mr. Clinton Foley knows that you intend to leave your property to his wife?"

"Certainly not," flared Cartright. "He doesn't know anything of the sort. He doesn't have to, does he?"

"No," Mason said, "I was just wondering, that's all."

"Well, he doesn't know it, and he's not going to know it," said Cartright.

"All right," Mason told him, "that's settled. How about the dog?"

"We've got to do something about that dog."

"What do you want to do?"

"I want Foley arrested."

"On what grounds?"

"On the grounds that he's driving me crazy. A man can't keep a dog like that. It's part of a deliberate plan of persecution. He knows how I feel about a howling dog. He's got that dog, and he's taught it to howl. The dog didn't used to howl, he's just started howling the last night or two. He's doing it to irritate me and to irritate his wife. His wife is sick in bed, and the dog howls. It means death in the neighborhood."

Cartright was speaking rapidly now, his eyes glittering feverishly, his hands gesticulating, aimlessly pawing at the air.

Mason pursed his lips.

"I think," he said slowly, "that I'm not going to be able to handle the matter for you, Cartright. I'm exceptionally busy right now. Just got out of court from a murder case, and . . ."

"I know, I know," said Cartright, "you think I'm crazy. You think it's just some little piece of business. I tell you it isn't. It's one of the biggest pieces of business you ever handled. I came to you because you have been trying that murder case. I've followed it. I've been in court listening to you. You're a real lawyer. You were one jump ahead of the district attorney in that case from the time it started. I know all about it."

Perry Mason smiled slowly.

"Thanks for your good opinion, Cartright," he said, "but you can understand my work is mostly trial work. I have specialized on trials. Drawing a will is not exactly in my line, and this matter of the howling dog seems to be something that can be adjusted without a lawyer. . . ."

"No, it can't," Cartright said. "You don't know Foley. You don't know the type of a man you're dealing with. Probably you think there isn't going to be enough money in it to pay you for your time, but I'm going to pay you. I'm going to pay you well."

He reached in his pocket, pulled out a well-filled wallet, opened it and jerked out three bills with trembling hand. He started to hand the bills to the lawyer, but they slipped from his fingers when his hand was half way across the desk, and fluttered to the blotter.

"There's three hundred dollars," he said. "That's for retainer. There'll be more when you get finished—lot3 more. I haven't been to the bank and got my cash yet, but I'm going to get it. I've got it in a safety deposit box— lots of it."

Perry Mason didn't touch the money for a moment. The tips of his firm capable fingers were drumming noiselessly on the desk.

"Cartright," he said slowly, "if I act as your lawyer in this thing, I am going to do what I think is for your own good and for your best interests, do you understand that?"

"Of course I understand it, that's what I want you to do."

"No matter what it is," warned Mason, " if I think it'3 for your best interests I'm going to do it."

"That's all right," Cartright told him, "if you'll just agree to handle the thing for me."

Perry Mason picked up the three one hundred dollar bills, folded them, put them in his pocket.

"Very well," he said, "I'll handle it for you. Now you want Foley arrested, is that right?"

"Yes."

"All right," Mason said, "that isn't going to be particularly complicated. You simply swear to a complaint, and the magistrate issues a warrant of arrest. Now, why did you want to retain me in that connection? Did you want me to act as special prosecutor?"

"You don't know Clinton Foley," doggedly repeated Arthur Cartright. "He'll come back at me. He'll file a suit against me for malicious prosecution. Perhaps he's just trained the dog to howl so that he can get me to walk into a trap."

"What kind of a dog is it?" Mason asked.

"A big police dog."

Perry Mason lowered his eyes and watched the tips of his drumming fingers for a moment, then looked up at Cartright with a reassuring smile.

"Legally," he said, "it's always a good defense to a suit for malicious prosecution if a person consults an attorney in good faith and puts all of the facts before him and then acts on the advice of that attorney. Now I'm going to put you in a position where no one can ever recover in a suit for malicious prosecution. I'm going to take you to a deputy in the district attorney's office, one who has charge of such matters. I'm going to let you talk with that deputy and tell him the whole story,—about the dog I mean. You don't need to tell him anything about the will. If he decides that a warrant should be issued, that's all there is to it. But I must warn you to tell the whole story to the district attorney. That is, give him all of the facts. State them fairly and completely, and then you'll have a perfect defense to any suit Foley might file."

Cartright sighed his relief.

"Now," he said, "you're talking sense. That's just exactly the kind of advice I want to pay for. Where do we find this deputy district attorney?"

"I'll have to telephone for an appointment," said Mason. "If you'll excuse me for a moment, I'll go see if I can get him on the telephone. Sit right here and make yourself at home. You'll find cigarettes there in the case, and . . ."

"Never mind that," Cartright said, making a swift motion toward his pocket, "I've got my own cigarettes here. Go right ahead and get that appointment. Let's do it right now. Let's get it over with as soon as possible. I can't stand another night of that howling dog."

"All right," Mason said, pushed back his swivel chair and walked to the door which led to the outer office. As his powerful shoulders swung the door back, Arthur Cartright was lighting a second cigarette with a hand that quivered so it was necessary for him to steady it with the other hand.

Mason walked into the outer office.

Della Street, his secretary, twenty-seven, swiftly capable, looked up at him and smiled with the intimacy which comes from thorough understanding.

"Cuckoo?" she said.

"I don't know," Perry Mason said; "I'm going to find out. Get me Pete Dorcas on the telephone. I'm going to put the whole deal up to him."

The girl nodded. Her fingers whirred the dial of a telephone into swift action. Perry Mason strode to a window and stood with his feet planted far apart, his broad shoulders blotting out the light, his eyes staring moodily down into the concrete canyon from which came the blaring sounds of automobile horns, the rumble of traffic. The afternoon light, striking his rugged features, gave the face a weatherbeaten appearance.

"Here he is," said Della Street.

Perry Mason turned, took two rapid strides, scooped up a telephone from a desk in the corner of the room, as Della Street's capable fingers plugged the call in on that line.

"Hello, Pete," said Mason. "This is Perry Mason. I'm

bringing a man down to see you, and I want to explain it to you in advance."

Pete Dorcas had a rasping, high-pitched voice, the voice of an office lawyer who has perfected himself in the mastery of technicalities, and is constantly explaining them to others who require argument in order to become convinced.

"Congratulations, Perry, on your victory. It was well thought out. I told the trial deputy there was a weak point in that case on the time element, and I warned him that if he went before a jury and couldn't explain that call about the stolen automobile, he'd lose his case."

"Thanks," said Mason laconically. "I get the breaks, that's all."

"Yes, you do," said Dorcas. "You make the breaks, that's why you get them. It suits me all right. I told these fellows they were skating on thin ice. Now how about this man that you're bringing down? What does he want?"

"He wants a complaint."

"On what?"

"On a howling dog."

"On a what?"

"That's right, a howling dog. I think there's a county ordinance against keeping a dog that howls in any congested area, whether it's incorporated as a city or not."

"There is some such ordinance; nobody pays any attention to it. That is, I've never had anything to do under it."

"All right," Mason said, "this is different. My client is either going crazy, or has gone crazy."

"On account of the howling dog?" asked Dorcas.

"I don't know; that's what I want to find out. If he's in need of treatment, I want him to have treatment. If he's worked up to the verge of a nervous collapse, I want to see that he gets a break. You understand that a howling dog might be just annoying to one person, and might drive a man of another temperament into insanity."

10

"I take it," Dorcas said, "you're going to bring him down here?"

"Yes, I'm going to bring him down there, and I want you to have a doctor present; one of the alienists who sits on insanity cases. Don't introduce him as a doctor, but introduce him as an assistant of some sort, and let him hear the conversation and perhaps ask a question or two. Then, if this man needs medical treatment, let's see that he gets it."

"Suppose he doesn't want it?"

"I said," Mason remarked, "that we should see that he gets it."

"You'd have to sign a complaint and have a commitment issued in order to do that," Dorcas pointed out.

"I know that," Mason said. "I'm willing to sign a complaint, myself, if the man needs medical treatment. I want to know, that's all. If he's crazy, I want to do what's best for him. If he isn't, I want to see that he gets action right away. I'm trying to represent his best interests, do you get me?"

"I got you," Dorcas remarked.

"Be there in fifteen minutes," said Mason, and hung up.

He was putting on his hat as he opened the door of the inner office, and nodded to Cartright.

"All right," he said, "he's waiting for us in the office. Have you got a car, or do we go in a taxicab?"

"We go in a taxicab," Cartright told him. "I'm too nervous to drive."

CHAPTER II

PETE DORCAS uncoiled his lean length from behind a battered desk, stared at Arthur Cartright with steely eyes, and acknowledged Perry Mason's introduction with the usual formula of pleasure. He half turned and indicated a short, paunchy individual, whose face held what seemed, at first glance, to be merely bubbling good nature. Only a second glance disclosed the wary watchfulness which lurked back of the twinkle in the gray eyes.

"Meet Mr. Cooper," he said, "my assistant."

The paunchy individual smiled his pleasure, came forward and shook hands with Cartright. The twinkling eyes studied Cartright's face in swift appraisal. The man held Cartright's hand for an appreciable interval after he had completed the perfunctory handshake.

"Well," said Mason, "I guess we're all ready to go; is that right?"

"All ready," said Dorcas, sitting down back of his desk.

He was tall, lean, high-cheeked and bald-headed, and there was a mental alertness about him which made his audience restless.

"It's about a dog," said Perry Mason. "Clinton Foley, residing at 4889 Milpas Drive, his house adjoining that of Mr. Cartright here, has a police dog that howls."

"Well," said Dorcas, grinning, "if a dog is entitled to one bite, he should be entitled to one howl."

Arthur Cartright did not smile. His hand shot to his pocket, pulled out a package of cigarettes, then, after a moment's hesitation, dropped the package back in the pocket.

Cooper's twinkling eyes, watching Cartright in constant appraisal, lost their expression of bubbling good humor for a moment, then once more started to twinkle.

"This man has got to be arrested," said Cartright. "The howling has got to be stopped. You hear? It's *got* to be stopped!"

"Sure," said Perry Mason, "that's what we're here for, Cartright. Go ahead and tell them your story."

"There's no story to tell; the dog howls, that's all."

"Constantly?" asked Cooper.

"Constantly. That is, I don't mean constantly, I mean he howls regularly at intervals, you know the way a dog howls. Damn it! No dog howls all the time. He howls, and then he stops, and then he howls again."

"What makes him howl?" asked Cooper.

"Foley makes him howl," said Cartright positively.

"And why?" asked Cooper.

"Because he knows it gets my goat. Because he knows it gets his wife's goat. It means a death in the neighborhood, and his wife is sick. I tell you he's got to stop it! That dog has got to be stopped."

Dorcas thumbed through the index of a leather-backed book, then said in a querulous, high-pitched voice:

"Well, there's an ordinance against it, an ordinance providing that if any one keeps any dog, cow, horse, chickens, rooster, guinea hen, fowl, animal or other livestock of any sort, nature or description within a congested area whether the same be incorporated or unincorporated, under such circumstances that a nuisance is created, it is a misdemeanor."

"What more do you want?" asked Cartright.

Dorcas laughed.

"*I* don't want any more of anything," he said. "Personally I don't like howling dogs and I don't like crowing roosters. This ordinance was originally enacted to keep dairies and livery stables out of the congested districts. Milpas Drive is an exclusive residential district. There's some rather expensive homes out there. What's your address, Mr. Cartright?"

"4893."

"And Foley's place is 4889?"

"That's right."

"Yet the two houses adjoin?"

"That's right."

"You've got rather a large lot?"

"He has."

"How about you?"

"Mine's just about average."

"Foley's wealthy?" asked Dorcas.

"Does that make any difference?" asked Cartright irri-

13

tably. "Of course, he's wealthy, or he wouldn't be living out there."

"It doesn't make a difference in one sense of the word," said Dorcas slowly, "but you understand we have to use our judgment here in the office. I don't like to send out and arrest a reputable citizen, without first giving him a warning. Suppose I give him a warning?"

"It won't do any good," said Cartright.

Perry Mason spoke slowly, with almost judicial dignity.

"My client," he said, "wants to be fair. You can use your judgment as to methods, Dorcas, but I am going to insist that the nuisance be abated, that the howling of the dog cease. You can see for yourself that my client is in a nervous condition. It's been brought about by the howling of the dog."

"I'm not nervous," snapped Cartright, "just a little upset, that's all."

Perry Mason nodded without saying anything. Cooper's eyes flickered to those of Mason, and his head gave an almost perceptible nod. Then the eyes swung back to Cartright.

"I think," said Dorcas slowly, "that the policy of the office would be not to prosecute until after we had given a warning. We'd write a letter to Mr. Foley, telling him that complaint had been made, and calling his attention to the county ordinance which makes the maintenance of such a dog a nuisance. We could tell him that if the dog is ill, or something, he should be confined in a hospital or kennel until after the attack has ceased."

Perry Mason glanced at Cartright, who started to say something, but was interrupted by Dorcas.

"The dog has been there for some time, Mr. Cartright?"

"Yes."

"How long?"

"I don't know—two months that I know of. I've only been there two months, myself. The dog has been there that long."

14

"And he hasn't howled before?"

"No."

"When did it start?"

"Night before last."

"I take it," said Dorcas, "that you're not on good terms with Foley. That is, you wouldn't run across and tell him to please make the animal stop howling?"

"No, I wouldn't do that."

"How about telephoning him?"

"No."

"Well, suppose I write him a letter?"

"You don't know Foley," said Cartright bitterly. "He'd tear the letter up and make the dog howl all the worse. He'd laugh with fiendish glee to think that he'd got my goat. He'd take the letter and show it to his wife, and . . ."

Cartright ceased speaking abruptly.

"Don't stop," said Dorcas. "Go on. What else would he do?"

"Nothing," said Cartright in a surly tone of voice.

"I think," said Mason, "that we will be content if you write the letter, Mr. Dorcas, with the understanding that if the dog doesn't quit howling, a warrant will be issued."

"Of course, there'll be that understanding," said the deputy district attorney.

"Now, a letter sent in the ordinary course of mail wouldn't be delivered until some time tomorrow, even if you got it out this afternoon," Mason said. "I am suggesting that you make a formal notification and send it out by one of the officers. Let the officer make a service upon Mr. Foley, personally, or upon any one else who may be in charge of the house, in the event Foley is not at home. This will have the effect of showing Foley that it is not merely a complaint instigated by Cartright, and having no legal status."

Cartright shook his head doggedly.

"I want him arrested," he said.

Perry Mason's tone was patient.

"You put the matter in my hands, Mr. Cartright," he said, "and you will remember what I told you. You, yourself, have stated that Foley is vindictive; that he is wealthy, and that he may start some action against you. If that happens, it is incumbent on you to show that you have acted throughout in the utmost good faith. I think that this step suggested by Mr. Dorcas, with the modifications in procedure which I have pointed out, will place you in the clear, legally. It is my advice that you follow that procedure."

Cartright whirled on Perry Mason with a display of temper.

"What if I don't choose to follow that advice?" he asked.

"Under those circumstances," said Perry Mason patiently, "you would, of course, prefer to get some other attorney—some one in whose advice you *would* have confidence."

Cartright paused for a moment, then suddenly nodded.

"Very well," he said, "I will be willing to follow that procedure. I want you to send the notification out right away, however."

"Just as soon as it can be prepared," said Perry Mason soothingly.

"Well, then," Cartright said, "I'm going to leave that up to you. I'm going back home. You represent my interests, Mr. Mason. You stay here and assist in getting out the proper notification, and seeing that it is delivered. Will you do that?"

"I will do that," said Perry Mason. "You can go home and get some rest, Cartright. Leave the matter in my hands."

Cartright nodded and paused with his hand on the door.

"Thank you, gentlemen," he said. "I am glad I met you. Pardon me if I seem a little upset. I haven't been sleeping much."

Then the door slammed.

"Well," said Pete Dorcas, turning to Dr. Cooper.

Dr. Cooper placed the tips of his fingers togther over his paunchy stomach.

"Well," he said, the twinkle abruptly fading from his eyes, "I wouldn't want to make a diagnosis on the limited evidence available at the present time, but I should say it was a case of manic depressive psychosis."

Perry Mason grinned.

"Sounds formidable, Doctor," he said, "but doesn't that mean merely a nervous breakdown?"

"There is no such thing," said Dr. Cooper, "as a nervous breakdown. It is a popular expression, applied to various forms of functional or degenerative psychoses."

"Well," said Mason, "let's get at it another way. A man who is suffering from a manic depressive psychosis isn't insane, is he?"

"He isn't normal."

"I know, but he isn't insane."

"Well, it's a question of what you mean by insane. It isn't, of course, the degree of legal insanity which would excuse one from committing a crime, if that's what you mean."

"That isn't what I mean," said Mason. "Come on down to earth, Doctor; let's quit splitting hairs. You're not on the witness stand; you're just telling us. It's purely a functional disease, isn't it?"

"That's right."

"And curable?"

"Oh, yes, completely curable."

"All right," said Mason irritably, "let's get rid of that howling dog then."

"Of course," said Pete Dorcas, twisting a pencil in his fingers, "we haven't any one's word for the fact that the dog is howling, other than this man Cartright's unsupported statement."

"Oh, forget it," Mason told him. "You're not getting out a warrant. Go ahead and make a notification to Clin-

17

ton Foley, stating that complaint has been made that he's violating ordinance number so and so, and give him a general idea of what the ordinance contains. He'll shut up the howling dog if he's got one, and if he hasn't he'll telephone in and let you know."

Mason turned to Dr. Cooper.

"That idea of the howling dog isn't apt to be a delusion, is it, Doctor?"

"They have delusions in manic depressive psychosis," said Dr. Cooper, "but usually they are delusions of persecution."

"Well," Dorcas remarked, "he thinks he's being persecuted. He thinks the dog is being put up to it by Foley."

Perry Mason looked at his watch.

"Let's get in a stenographer," he said, "and we can dictate a notice that will cover the case, and get it dispatched."

Dorcas turned to Dr. Cooper and raised his eyebrows.

Dr. Cooper nodded.

Dorcas pushed a button with his forefinger.

"Very well," he said, "I'll dictate it and sign it."

"I want to talk with the deputy who's going to take it out," said Mason. "I can perhaps expedite matters a little by seeing that he has ample transportation provided, and . . ."

Dorcas grinned.

"You mean giving him a few cigars," he said.

"Perhaps," Perry Mason said, "I might give him a bottle, but I wouldn't want to commit myself in front of a deputy district attorney."

"Go on down to the sheriff's office," said Dorcas, "and get a deputy assigned to deliver the notice. I'll have it ready by the time you get back. You can go out with the deputy if you want to."

"Not me," Mason said, grinning. "I know the proper place for a lawyer and the proper place for a deputy sheriff. One's in the office and the other's on the ground, delivering notices. I'll be in my office when the notice is delivered."

He opened the door of the office and turned to Dr. Cooper. "Don't think I'm argumentative, Doctor. I appreciate the position you're in, but I hope you appreciate the position I'm in. This man came into the office, and I could see that he was in a nervous condition. I didn't know whether he was insane or not. I wanted to find out."

"Of course," Dr. Cooper said, "I can't make a complete diagnosis. . . ."

"I understand that," Mason told him.

"Did he say anything else?" asked Dorcas. "Did he want to consult you about anything other than the howling dog?"

Perry Mason smiled, a slow, patient smile.

"Now," he said, "you *are* asking questions. I can tell you, however, that the man paid me a retainer, if that will be of any help?"

"In cash?" asked Dorcas.

"In cash."

"That settles it," said Dr. Cooper, laughing, "a certain sign of insanity—a departure from the normal."

"I'll say it's a departure from the normal," Perry Mason remarked, and closed the door behind him.

CHAPTER III

DELLA STREET had Perry Mason's morning mail opened when he pushed open the door of the outer office with a cheery "Good morning. What's new, Della?"

"A lot of the usual stuff," she said, "and one that isn't usual."

"We'll save the cake until last," he told her, grinning. "What's the usual stuff?"

"One of the jurors on that last case," she said, "wants to talk over a corporation matter with you. A couple more rang up to congratulate you on the way you handled the case. There's a man who's been trying to get an appointment and won't tell me the details of what it's about. It's got something to do with some mining stock he bought. There are letters asking about minor matters. . . ."

He made a wry face and a sweeping gesture of dismissal with his hand, then grinned at her.

"Kick 'em all out, Della," he said. "I don't like routine. I want excitement. I want to work on matters of life and death, where minutes count. I want the bizarre and the unusual."

She looked at him with eyes that held a tender solicitude. "You take too many chances, Chief," she protested. "Your love of excitement is going to get you into trouble some day. Why don't you simply handle trial work instead of going out and mixing into the cases the way you do?"

His grin was boyish.

"In the first place," he said, "I like the excitement. In the second place, because I win my cases by knowing the facts. I beat the prosecution to the punch. It's lots of fun. . . . What's the unusual thing, Della?"

"That's *plenty* unusual, Chief," she said. "It's a letter from this man who was in here yesterday."

"What man?"

"The man who wanted to see you about the howling dog."

"Oh," said Mason, grinning, "Cartright, eh? Wonder if he slept last night."

"This letter," she reported, "came special delivery. It must have been mailed some time during the night."

"Something more about the dog?" he asked.

"He enclosed a will," she said, lowering her voice and looking furtively about the outer office as though afraid that some one might overhear her, "and ten one thousand dollar bills."

Perry Mason stood staring down at her with his forehead washboarded, his eyes squinted.

"You mean ten thousand dollars in currency?" he asked.

"Yes," she said.

"Sent through the mail?"

"Through the mail."

"Registered?"

"No, just special delivery."

"I," said Perry Mason, "will be damned."

She got up from behind the desk, walked over to the safe, opened the safe, unlocked the inner compartment, and took out the envelope and handed it to him.

"And you say there's a will?"

"A will."

"A letter with it?"

"Yes, a short letter."

Perry Mason fished out the ten one thousand dollar bills, looked them over carefully, whistled under his breath, folded them and put them in his pocket. Then he read the letter aloud.

"DEAR MR. MASON:

I saw you during that last murder trial. I'm convinced you're honest and I'm convinced you're a fighter. I want you to fight on this case. I'm enclosing ten thousand dollars and I'm enclosing a will. The ten thousand dollars is a retainer. You get your fee under the will. I want you to represent the beneficiary named in that will and fight for her interests all the way through. I know now why the dog howled.

I'm drawing up this will, the way you told me a will like this could be made. Perhaps you won't have any occasion to probate the will or fight for the beneficiary. If you don't, you've got the ten thousand dollars, plus the retainer I gave you yesterday.

Thanks for the interest you've taken in my case.

Sincerely yours,
ARTHUR CARTRIGHT."

Perry Mason shook his head dubiously and took the folded bills from his pocket.

"I'd sure like to keep that money," he said.

"Keep it!" exclaimed Della Street. "Why, of course you'll keep it. The letter shows what it's for. It's a legitimate retainer, isn't it?"

Perry Mason sighed and dropped the money onto her desk.

"Crazy," he said. "The man's crazy as a loon."

"What makes you think he's crazy?" she asked.

"Everything," he told her.

"You didn't think so last night."

"I thought he was nervous and perhaps sick."

"But you didn't think he was crazy."

"Well, not exactly."

"You mean the reason you think he's crazy, then, is because he sent you this letter."

Perry Mason grinned at her.

"Well," he said, "Dr. Charles Cooper, the alienist who handles the commitments on the insanity board, remarked that the payment of a cash retainer was certainly a departure from the normal these days. This man has paid two of them within twenty-four hours, and he sent ten thousand dollars through the mail in an unregistered letter."

"Perhaps he didn't have any other way to send it," suggested Della Street.

"Perhaps," he told her. "Did you read the will?"

"No, I didn't. The letter came in, and when I saw what it was, I put it in the safe right away."

"Well," Mason told her, "let's take a look at the will."

He unfolded the sheet of paper which was marked on the outside: "LAST WILL OF ARTHUR CARTRIGHT."

His eye ran along the writing, and he slowly nodded.

"Well," he said, "he's made a good holographic will. It's all in his handwriting—signature, date and everything."

"Does he leave you something in the will?" asked Della Street curiously.

Perry Mason looked up from the paper and chuckled.

"My, but you're getting mercenary this morning," he said.

"If you could see the way bills keep coming in, you'd be mercenary too. Honestly, I don't see how there can be any depression, the way you spend money."

"I'm just keeping it in circulation," he told her. "There's just as much money in the country as there ever was—more in fact, but it doesn't circulate as rapidly. Therefore, nobody seems to have any."

"Well," she told him, "yours circulates fast enough. But tell me about the will, or is it any of my business?"

"Oh, it's your business, all right," he told her. "One of these days I may get bumped off, the way I work up my cases, and you'll be the only one that knows anything about my business affairs. Let's see. He leaves his property to the beneficiary, and then he leaves me a one-tenth interest in his estate, to be paid to me when the estate is finally distributed, upon condition that I have faithfully represented the woman who is the principal beneficiary, in every form of legal matter which may arise, incident to the will, growing out of his death, or in anywise connected with her domestic relationships."

"Takes in a lot of territory, doesn't he?" said Della Street.

Perry Mason nodded his head slowly, and when he spoke, his voice was meditative.

"That man," he said, "either wrote that will at the dictation of a lawyer, or else he's got a pretty good business mind. It isn't the kind of a will a crazy man would write. It's logical and coherent. He leaves his property, nine-tenths to Mrs. Clinton Foley, and one-tenth to me. He provides . . ."

Suddenly Perry Mason broke off and stared at the document with eyes that slowly widened in surprise.

"What is it?" asked Della Street. "Anything serious; a defect in the will?"

"No," said Mason slowly, "it's not a defect in the will, but it's something peculiar."

Abruptly he strode across the office to the door which opened into the outer corridor, and locked it.

"We're not going to bother with visitors for a while, Della," he told her, "not until we get this straightened out."

"But what is it?" she asked.

Perry Mason lowered his voice.

"Yesterday," he said, "when the man was in, he asked me particularly about leaving the property to Mrs. Clinton Foley, and wanted to know what the effect of the will would be if it should turn out that the woman who posed as Mrs. Foley, wasn't really Mrs. Foley."

"Meaning that she wasn't married to Clinton Foley?" asked Della Street.

"Exactly," said Mason.

"But isn't she living with Mr. Foley out there in an exclusive neighborhood?"

"Exactly," Mason said, "but that doesn't prove anything. There have been cases where . . ."

"Oh, yes, I know," said Della Street. "But it does seem strange that a man would live in a neighborhood like that with a woman who *posed* as his wife."

"There might be reasons for it. Those things happen every day. Perhaps a former wife who won't get a divorce, herself, and won't let the man get one. Perhaps the woman has a husband. There might be any one of a dozen things."

She nodded slow affirmation. "You've got me curious now. What about the will?"

"Well," said Mason, "when he was in yesterday he brought up this question about leaving the property to Mrs. Clinton Foley if it should turn out that the woman wasn't Mrs. Clinton Foley at all, but was merely posing

24

as Mrs. Foley. From the way he spoke, I felt quite certain that he had reason to believe the woman was not Mrs. Foley, so I explained to him that it would be all right for him to leave the property to the party named, describing her as being the woman who at present resided with Clinton Foley, at 4889 Milpas Drive."

"Well," asked Della Street, "did he do it?"

"He did not," said Perry Mason. "He left his property to Mrs. Clinton Foley, the lawfully wedded wife of Clinton Foley, said Clinton Foley at present residing at 4889 Milpas Drive in this city.

"Then that makes it different?" asked Della Street.

"Of course it makes it different," he said. "It makes it different all the way through. If it should turn out that the woman who is living with him at that address isn't his wife, she wouldn't take under the will. The will distributes the property to the lawfully wedded wife of Clinton Foley, and the description of the residence relates to Clinton Foley rather than his wife."

"Do you suppose he misunderstood you?" asked Della Street.

"I don't know," frowned the lawyer. "He didn't seem to misunderstand me on anything else, and he's been clear enough in everything he's done. Look up Cartright in the telephone book. He lives at 4893 Milpas Drive. He'll have a telephone. Get him on the telephone at once. Tell him it's important."

She nodded and reached for the telephone, but an incoming call tripped the buzzer on the switchboard before her fingers closed about the receiver.

"See who it is," said Mason.

She plugged in the line, said: "Office of Perry Mason," then listened for a moment, and nodded.

"Just a minute," she said, and cupped her palm over the mouthpiece.

"It's Pete Dorcas," she said, "the deputy district attorney. He says he wants to talk to you right away about that Cartright case."

"All right," said Mason, "put him on."

"In your office?" she asked.

"No, this telephone's all right," he told her, "and listen in on the conversation. I don't know just what it's going to be, but I want a witness."

He scooped up the receiver, said "Hello," and heard the voice of Pete Dorcas, edged with impatience, querulous and rasping.

"I'm afraid, Mason," he said, "that I've got to issue a commitment for your client, Arthur Cartright, on the ground of insanity."

"What's he done now?" asked Mason.

"Apparently this howling dog business is all a part of his imagination," Dorcas said. "Clinton Foley has told me enough to make me believe that the man is not only dangerously insane, but that he has a homicidal complex which may cause him to take the law in his own hands and become violent."

"When did Foley tell you all this?" Mason asked, looking at his wristwatch.

"Just a few minutes ago."

"He was there at the office?" asked Mason.

"He's here right now."

"All right," Mason said, "hold him there. I've got a right to be heard on this. I'm Cartright's lawyer, and I'm going to see that my client gets a square deal. You hold him there. I'm coming right over."

He didn't wait to give Dorcas a chance to make any excuses, but slammed the receiver back on the telephone, turned and said to Della Street: "All right, Della, break that connection. Get Cartright on the line. Tell him that I want to see him at once. Tell him to get out of his house and go to some hotel; register under his own name, but don't let any one know where he's going; telephone you the name of the hotel where he's at, and you can telephone me. Tell him to keep away from my office and keep away from his residence until I see him. Tell him it's important. I'm going over to the district attorney's office and see what's happening. This Clinton Foley is making trouble."

He slipped back the spring lock on the outer door, shot out into the corridor and was half way to the elevator by the time the door check swung the door shut, and the spring latch snapped into position.

He flagged a cab in front of his office and snapped at the driver: "District attorney's office. Make it snappy and I pay the fines."

He jumped into the cab, the door slammed, and Perry Mason lurched back against the cushions as the cab lunged into motion. During the drive, he sat with his eyes staring, unseeingly, straight ahead, his forehead puckered with thought. His body swayed mechanically as the cab swung around corners or lurched from side to side in avoiding obstacles.

When the cab swung into the curb and the driver pulled the slip from the meter, Perry Mason tossed him a five dollar bill and said: "That's all right, buddy." He crossed the sidewalk, went to the ninth floor, said to the girl at the information desk in the district attorney's office: "Pete Dorcas is waiting for me."

He walked past her, down a long corridor lined with doors, paused before one that had gilt letters on the frosted glass, reading simply: "Mr. Dorcas," and tapped on the door.

The querulous voice of Pete Dorcas called: "Come in."

Perry Mason turned the knob and walked into the room.

Pete Dorcas was sitting behind the desk, an expression of annoyance on his face. On the other side of the desk, a huge figure struggled from a chair and turned to face Perry Mason inquiringly.

The man was over six feet in height, broad of shoulder, deep of chest, long of arm. His waist had put on a little flesh, but not enough to detract from the athletic figure. He was, perhaps, forty years old, and when he spoke, his voice was resonant.

"I presume you're Perry Mason," he said, "Mr. Cartright's lawyer?"

Perry Mason nodded curtly, stood with his feet spread apart, his head thrust slightly forward, his eyes staring at the man in cold appraisal.

"Yes," he said, "I'm Cartright's lawyer."

"I'm Mr. Clinton Foley, his neighbor," said the man, extending a hand and smiling graciously.

Perry Mason took two steps forward, took the hand, and turned to Dorcas after a perfunctory handshake.

"Sorry if I kept you waiting, Pete, but this is important. I can explain it to you a little later. I've got to find out what it's all about."

"There's nothing that it's all about," said Dorcas, "except that I'm busy, and you took up a lot of my time yesterday afternoon about a howling dog who didn't howl, and now it turns out your man's crazy as a loon."

"What makes you think he's crazy?" asked Mason.

"What made *you* think he was crazy?" said Dorcas irritably. "You thought so yesterday. You telephoned and said you thought he was crazy and wanted me to have a doctor here to look him over."

"No," Mason said slowly, "don't get me wrong on that, Dorcas. I knew the man was in a very bad state of nerves. I wanted to find out whether that was all there was to it, that's all."

"Yes, you did," Dorcas said, with heavy sarcasm. "You thought he was crazy, and you wanted to find out before you got your neck in a noose."

"What do you mean, get my neck in a noose?" demanded Mason.

"You know what I mean," Dorcas told him. "You came in here with a man who wanted to get out a warrant for the arrest of a wealthy and prominent citizen. Naturally,

28

you wanted to be certain that there wasn't going to be any come-back. That's what you were retained for. That's the reason you didn't get a warrant, but did get a notification asking Mr. Foley to come in. Well, he's here now, and what he tells me is plenty."

Perry Mason stared fixedly at Pete Dorcas until the steely eyes of the deputy district attorney lowered under Mason's direct gaze.

"When I came in here," Mason said slowly, "I came in here because I wanted to give you a fair deal, and because I wanted to get one. I told you my man was nervous. He told me he was nervous. He said the continued howling of the dog made him nervous. There's an ordinance on the books against maintaining a nuisance with a noisy animal. My client is entitled to the protection of that law, even if it does happen that a man who's got some political pull . . ."

"But the dog didn't howl," Dorcas exclaimed irritably. "That's just the point."

Foley's voice interposed on the discussion.

"Pardon me, gentlemen," he said, "may I say a word?"

Perry Mason didn't even turn to him, but continued to stare steadily at the deputy district attorney. Dorcas, however, looked up, his face showing relief.

"Certainly," he said, "go right ahead."

"You'll pardon me, I'm certain, Mr. Mason," said Foley, "if I speak frankly. I know that you want to get at the facts. I understand your position in this matter and want to commend you upon the fair way you have gone about protecting the interests of your client."

Perry Mason turned slowly toward him, sized him up with uncordial eyes that swept up and down the big frame of the man.

"Forget it," he said, "go ahead and explain."

"This man, Cartright," said Foley, "is undoubtedly mentally deranged. He has rented the adjoining house. I feel quite certain that the owners of the house do not know the sort of tenant with whom they are dealing. Cartright has one servant, a deaf housekeeper. He has no friends, apparently; no acquaintances. He stays around his house virtually all of the time."

"Well," said Perry Mason belligerently, "that's his privilege, isn't it? Maybe he doesn't like the neighborhood."

Dorcas got to his feet.

"Now listen, Mason," he said, "you can't . . ."

"Gentlemen, *please*," said Foley. "Let me explain. Let me handle this. Please, Mr. Dorcas. I understand Mr. Mason's attitude. He thinks that I have brought political influence to bear, and that the interests of his client are being jeopardized."

"Well," said Mason, "haven't you?"

"No," said Foley, smiling amiably. "I have merely explained the facts to Mr. Dorcas. Your client, as I have said, is a very peculiar man. He lives virtually the life of a hermit, yet he continually spies on me out of the windows of his house, he has a pair of binoculars, and he watches every move I make."

Dorcas hesitated for a moment, then dropped back into his swivel chair, shrugged his shoulders, and lit a cigarette.

"Go on," said Perry Mason, "I'm listening."

"My Chinese cook," said Foley, "was the one who first called it to my attention. He noticed the lenses of the binoculars. Understand me, please, Mr. Mason. I consider only that your client is mentally deranged and doesn't know what he is doing. Also, please understand that I have ample witnesses to substantiate everything I am going to say."

"All right," said Mason, "what are you going to say?"

"I am going," Foley said, with dignity, "to complain about the constant espionage. It makes it difficult for me to keep my servants. It is annoying to me and to my guests. The man snoops around and stares at me through binoculars. He never has the lights on the upper floor of his house turned on. He constantly parades through the dark rooms at night, with his binoculars in his hand, snooping and spying on everything that I do. He is a dangerous neighbor."

"Well," Mason said, "it's no crime for a man to look through binoculars, is it?"

"That isn't the point," Dorcas said, "and you know it, Mason. The man is insane."

"What makes you think he's insane?" Mason demanded.

"Because," said Dorcas, "he has reported a howling dog, and the dog didn't howl."

"You've got a dog, haven't you?" Mason asked Foley.

"Certainly," said Foley, still keeping his conciliatory manner.

"And you mean to say he doesn't howl?"

"Never."

"Didn't howl a couple of nights ago?"

"No."

"I've talked it over with Dr. Cooper," said Dorcas, "and he tells me that if there is a delusion of persecution, coupled with the hallucination of a howling dog, and the fear that there is going to be a death in the neighborhood, present in your client's mind, he may develop homicidal mania at almost any moment, and without warning."

"All right," Mason said; "your mind's made up. So's mine. You're going to commit him, are you?"

"I propose to see that his sanity is inquired into," said Dorcas, with dignity.

"Go ahead," Mason told him. "The same thing that you told me yesterday, I'm telling you today. If you're going to have a man's sanity inquired into, some one has got to sign a complaint. Now who's going to sign the complaint? Are you?"

"I might," Dorcas said.

"Better take it easy," Mason said; "I'm just warning you, that's all."

"Warning me of what?"

"Warning you that if you sign a complaint alleging that my client is insane, you'd better make a much more complete investigation than you've made to date. Otherwise there's going to be some trouble."

"Gentlemen, gentlemen," said Foley. "Please let's not have any friction about this. After all, it's merely a matter of doing the right thing by poor Mr. Cartright. I have no feelings against him whatever. He is a neighbor and he has made himself obnoxious, but I feel certain that his conduct is caused by a mental derangement. I desire to have that inquired into, that is all. In the event it appears the man's mind is not deranged, then I shall take steps, naturally, to see that he does not repeat his assertions about my dog and my household."

Dorcas spoke to Perry Mason.

"This isn't getting you anywhere, Perry," he said. "Foley's absolutely within his rights. You know that you brought Cartright here because you wanted to forestall any action for malicious prosecution. If Cartright made a full and complete disclosure of the facts to us, and was authorized to proceed, he acted within his rights. If he distorted or misstated the facts, he did not."

Mason laughed grimly.

"Trying to lay the foundation for a lawsuit, are you?" he asked Foley.

"I am not," Foley said.

"Well, I'm just telling you both something that you've forgotten," Mason remarked, "and that is that no warrant was issued and no complaint was filed. The deputy district attorney decided to write you a letter. That's about the size of it, isn't it, Dorcas?"

"Legally, yes," said Dorcas slowly. "But if it appears the man is insane, something should be done about it."

"All right," Mason said, "all of your ideas about the man's insanity are founded on the statement Foley has made, that the dog didn't howl, isn't that right?"

"Naturally, but Mr. Foley says he has witnesses to substantiate his statement."

"So *he* says," Mason went on doggedly, "and until you interview those witnesses, you don't know which one of them is crazy. Maybe it's Foley that's crazy."

Foley laughed, but the laugh was mechanical, and his eyes glinted.

"Well, then," Dorcas said, "as I understand it, you want us to investigate further before we do anything, is that right?"

"Naturally," said Mason. "You didn't go any farther on the word of *my* client, than to write a letter. If you want to write Mr. Cartright a letter, telling him that Mr. Foley says he's crazy, that's all right with me. But if you go ahead on the unsupported word of Mr. Foley, I'm going to stick up for the rights of my client."

Dorcas reached for his desk phone, took down the receiver, and said:

"Sheriff's office."

After a moment, he said: "Let me talk with Bill Pemberton . . . hello . . . Bill? . . . this is Pete Dorcas. Listen, we've got a dispute down here in the office, involving a couple of millionaires out on Milpas Drive. There's a question of a howling dog. One of them says the dog howls; the other one says he doesn't. One of them says the other man's crazy. Perry Mason is retained to represent one of them and demands an investigation. Can you go out there and settle the thing?"

There was a moment of silence, then Dorcas said: "All right, come down to the office right away."

He hung up the telephone and turned to look at Perry Mason with cold eyes.

"Now, then, Perry," he said, "you've started this thing. We're going to make an investigation. If it turns out your man is making false statements, and is mentally deranged we're going to go right through with a commitment, unless

33

you want to find some relative and have the man committed privately."

"Now," said Mason, "you're commencing to talk sense. Why didn't you tell me that in the first place?"

"Tell you what?"

"Tell me that I could find a relative and get the man committed?"

"Well," said Dorcas, "he started the machinery of this office on a criminal matter which seems to have been entirely without foundation. Then Mr. Foley came in and impressed upon us the fact that his safety was being jeopardized. . . ."

"Exactly," said Perry Mason, "that's what I was combatting.

"There's no hard feelings, Pete, but I'm representing my client, and when I represent a client, I fight for him—to the last ditch if necessary."

Dorcas sighed and made a gesture with his hands, spreading them out, palm upward on the desk.

"That's one thing about you, Mason," he said, "nobody can ever say you don't represent a client. You're hard to get along with."

"Not when my clients get a square deal," Mason said.

"Your client will get a square deal here," Dorcas told him, "as long as I'm running things. Bill Pemberton is fair, and he's going out and make an investigation."

"I want to go with him," Mason stated.

"Can you go, Mr. Foley?" Dorcas asked.

"When?" asked Mr. Foley.

"Right away," said Mason. "The sooner, the better."

"Yes," said Foley slowly, "I can go."

A figure silhouetted against the frosted glass of the outer door, then the door pushed open, and a raw-boned man, of forty-five years of age, grinned goodnaturedly as he walked into the office.

"Hello, everybody," he said.

"Hello, Pemberton," Mason replied.

"Bill," said Dorcas, "shake hands with Mr. Foley. Mr. Foley is one of the parties to the controversy."

The deputy sheriff and Foley shook hands, and then Pemberton extended his hand to Mason.

"Great fight you made on that murder case, Mason," he said. "A nice piece of detective work. I want to compliment you on it."

"Thanks," Mason told him, shaking hands.

"What's this about?" Pemberton inquired of Dorcas.

"A howling dog," said the deputy district attorney, wearily.

"Making a lot of fuss over a howling dog, ain't you?" Pemberton asked. "Why not give him a piece of beefsteak and shut him up?"

"He's shut up already," Foley laughed. "That's the trouble."

"Foley will tell you the story on the way out," Dorcas said. "Foley represents one side of the controversy, and Perry represents the folks on the other side. It started out with a complaint over a howling dog, and now it's gone into a question of espionage, homicidal mania, and whatnot. Go on out and find out what it's all about. Talk with witnesses and then make a report to me. I'll take action, depending on what's disclosed by your report."

"Who are the witnesses?" Pemberton asked.

Foley held up his fingers and checked them off.

"To begin with," he said, "there's Cartright, who claims the dog howls, and Cartright's housekeeper. She may claim that she heard the dog howl, but if you'll talk with her, you'll find she's deaf as a post, and couldn't hear it thunder. Then there's my wife, who's been quite ill with influenza, but is getting better now. She's in bed, but she can talk with you. She knows the dog didn't howl. There's Ah Wong, my Chinese manservant, and Thelma Benton, my housekeeper. They can all tell you that the dog didn't howl. Then there's the dog himself."

"The dog going to tell me he didn't howl?" asked Pemberton, grinning.

"The dog can show you that he's quite contented, and that there isn't a howl in his system," smiled Foley, reaching in his pocket and taking out a leather cigar case. "How about a cigar?"

"Thanks," said Pemberton, taking a cigar.

"You?" asked Foley, extending the case to Mason.

"Thanks," said Mason, "I'll stick with my cigarettes."

"I've given this case a lot of time," said Dorcas, suggestively, "and . . ."

"Okay, Pete," Bill Pemberton boomed good-naturedly, "we're on our way right now. Come on, fellows."

CHAPTER IV

As the sheriff's car swung into the curb, Bill Pemberton said: "Is that the house?"

"That's it," Foley answered, "but don't park here. Go on in the driveway. I'm putting an addition onto my garage, and the contractors have got things littered up here. They're finishing up this afternoon, and then I won't be troubled with them. It's been a nuisance."

"Whom do we talk with first?" asked Pemberton.

"You can suit yourself," Foley said with dignity, "but I think that after you have talked with my wife, you won't need to bother with any more witnesses."

"No," Pemberton said, "we're going to see them all. How about the Chinese cook? Is he home?"

"Certainly," Foley answered. "Keep right on the driveway if you want to, and we'll have him come out to his room. You'll probably want to see where he sleeps. It's over the garage."

"You're building an addition on that?"

"On the garage, not on the room," Foley said. "It's only the one story. The cook has his apartments on top of the garage."

"How about a chauffeur?" asked Pemberton.

"I presume the place was originally intended as a chauffeur's apartment," Foley admitted, "but I don't keep a chauffeur. What driving I do, I do personally."

"Well, then," Pemberton said, "let's talk with the Chink. That suit you, Mason?"

"Anything suits me," said Mason. "Only I want to have you talk with my client before you go."

"Oh, sure. That his place over there, Foley?"

"That's it; the one on the north."

The car slid along the driveway and came to a stop in front of the building where men were laboring with a sudden zeal which indicated a desire to impress the owner of the property, and, perhaps, forestall any complaint as to the manner in which the work had dragged along.

"Just go up here," said Foley, "and I'll get Ah Wong."

Pemberton started up a flight of stairs which hugged the concrete side of the building, then paused as there was the sound of a door banging and a woman's voice said: "Oh, Mr. Foley, I must see you at once. We've had trouble. . . ."

The words became inaudible as the woman lowered her voice, on seeing the officer's car.

Bill Pemberton hesitated, then turned and walked toward the back of the residence.

"Something about the dog, Foley?" he asked.

"I don't know," Clinton Foley said.

A young woman, attired in a housedress and apron, with her right hand and arm bandaged, walked rapidly toward Foley.

She was, perhaps, twenty-seven or twenty-eight. Her hair was slicked back on her head. Her face was without make-up, and she gave the impression of homely efficiency, yet it would have needed but a few deft touches of make-up, a change of clothes, and a fingerwave, to have made her quite beautiful.

Bill Pemberton looked at her with narrowing eyes.

"My housekeeper," Foley explained.

"Oh," said Pemberton significantly.

Foley whirled, started to say something, then paused and waited until the woman came to him.

"What happened?" he asked.

"Prince bit me," she said. "He was sick."

"How did it happen?"

"I don't know, but I think he'd been poisoned. He was acting queerly. I remembered what you'd said about putting salt on the back of his tongue if he ever gave any sign of sudden illness, so I took a handful of salt and put it on the back of his tongue. He closed his teeth and bit me."

Foley looked at the bandaged hand.

"Bad?" he asked.

"No," she said, "I don't think so."

"Where is he now?"

"I shut him in your bedroom after the salt had done its work. But I thought you should know—about the poison I mean."

"Is he better now?"

"He seems to be all cured."

"Was he having spasms?"

"No, he was lying and shivering. I spoke to him two or three times, and he didn't seem to take any interest. He seemed in sort of a stupor."

Foley nodded, turned to Pemberton.

"Mrs. Benton," he said, "this is Mr. Pemberton, a deputy sheriff, and this is Mr. Perry Mason, a lawyer. These gentlemen are investigating a charge that has been made by neighbors."

"A charge by neighbors?" asked Mrs. Benton, stepping back, and letting her eyes grow wide with surprise.

"Yes, a charge that we're maintaining a nuisance here."

"How's that?" she inquired.

"About the dog," Foley said. "There's a claim made that . . ."

"Just a moment," said Pemberton. "Let me do the talking, please."

The young woman looked at Pemberton, then at Foley. Foley nodded, and Pemberton said: "This dog is a police dog whose name is Prince?"

"Yes, sir."

"And he lives here in the house?"

"Yes, sir, of course. He's Mr. Foley's dog."

"How long has he been here?"

"We've been here for about a year."

"And the dog has been with you all of that time?"

"Yes, sir."

"Now, has the dog been howling?"

"Howling? No, sir. He barked once yesterday when a peddler came to the door, but there hasn't been any howling."

"How about nights? Has he done any howling at night?"

"No, sir."

"Barking?"

"No, sir."

"You're certain about that?"

"Of course, I'm certain."

"Has the dog been acting strangely?"

"Well," she said, "he looked to me as though he'd been poisoned, and I tried to give him some salt. That's what Mr. Foley told me to do under those circumstances. Perhaps I shouldn't have done it. Perhaps he was just having some sort of a spasm, but . . ."

"That isn't what I mean," said Pemberton. "I mean has the dog shown any unusual symptoms, aside from this matter of poisoning?"

"No, sir."

Pemberton turned to Perry Mason.

"Suppose there's any chance this client of yours tried to poison the dog, Mason?"

"Not a chance in the world," said Perry Mason positively.

"Understand," said Foley hastily, "*I'm* not making any

accusations against Mr. Cartright. I don't think he's the type that would poison a dog—however, he's really not responsible."

"Well," said the young woman positively, "I don't know where he got it from, but somebody gave him some poison. I'm willing to swear to that. He was a sick dog until after I gave him the salt, and then he got better."

"What does salt do?" asked Pemberton of Foley.

"It's a powerful and immediate emetic," Foley said.

Pemberton looked back at the girl.

"And you're willing to swear that the dog hasn't been howling?"

"Of course I am."

"If he had howled, would you have heard him?"

"Yes."

"Where do you sleep, in the house?"

"Yes, on the upper floor."

"And who else is in the house?"

"There's Ah Wong, the cook, but he sleeps out over the garage. And then there's Mrs. Foley."

"I think, officer," said Foley, "that it will, perhaps, be better for you to talk with my wife, and she can tell you . . ."

"I beg your pardon," said Mrs. Benton, "I didn't want to tell you in front of these gentlemen, but your wife isn't here."

Foley stared at her with eyes that showed incredulous surprise.

"Isn't here?" he said. "Good heavens, girl, she couldn't have gone out! She's recovering from influenza."

"Nevertheless, she went out," said Mrs. Benton.

"How did she go? The cars aren't gone."

"In a taxi."

"Good heavens!" said Foley. "The woman will kill herself. What's the idea of going out when she's just recovering from influenza?"

"I don't know, sir."

"Did she say where she was going? Was she going shopping, calling, or what? Did she receive any messages? Was there something urgent? Come on, speak up! Don't be so mysterious."

"She left you a note, sir."

"A note?"

"Yes."

"Where is it?"

"Upstairs in her room. She left it on the dresser and asked me to see that you received it."

Foley stood staring at the woman, his forehead puckered, his eyes suddenly hard.

"Look here," he said, "you're keeping something from me."

The young housekeeper lowered her eyes.

"She took a suitcase with her," she said.

"A suitcase?" Foley exclaimed. "Was she going to a hospital?"

"I don't know. She didn't say. She simply left the note."

Foley looked at the deputy sheriff.

"May I be excused for a moment?" he asked.

"Certainly," said Pemberton, "go right ahead."

Foley strode into the house. Perry Mason looked at Mrs. Benton, studying her face closely.

"Was there," he asked, "some trouble between you and Mrs. Foley immediately prior to her departure?"

The young woman drew herself up and stared at him in haughty insolence.

"I don't know who you are," she said, "but I do know that I don't have to answer your absurd questions or your dirty insinuations," and she turned and flounced into the house.

Pemberton grinned over at Perry Mason and bit the end off a cigar.

"That," he said, "for you."

"The girl's tried to make herself up as ugly as possible," Mason said, frowning, "but she's rather young to be a housekeeper, and there's just a chance that while Mrs. Foley was ill in bed, there might have been some developments which brought about the woman's sudden departure."

"Not gossiping, are you, Mason?" asked Pemberton.

"No," said Mason gravely, "I'm speculating, that's all."

"Why speculate?"

"Because," said Perry Mason, "when a man makes an accusation against my client, claiming my client's insane, that man has got to be prepared to have a fight on his hands."

The back door opened, and Mrs. Benton came out.

"I'm sorry," she said. "Mr. Foley wants you to come in. I shouldn't have got mad and walked away. Will you excuse it?"

"Don't mention it," said Bill Pemberton. "The fault was ours," and he looked at Perry Mason.

"I came out here," said Perry Mason, "to get information, and to see that my client had a square deal."

"No," said Bill Pemberton slowly, "*we* came out here to see if the dog had been howling. That's about as far as I figure we're going to pry into the situation here."

Perry Mason said nothing.

The young woman led them through the back door, into a kitchen. A small, slender Chinese, attired in a cook apron, regarded them with glittering, beady eyes.

"Whassa malla?" he asked.

"We're trying to find out about the dog . . ." Perry Mason began, but was interrupted by Pemberton.

"Just a moment, Mason, please," he said; "let me handle this. I understand handling these Chinks pretty well."

"What's your name?" he asked.

"Ah Wong."

"You cook here?"

"I cook."

"You savvy him one piecie dog?"

42

"Heap savvy."

"You hear dog makum noise? Hearum make howl at night?"

The Chinese shook his head slowly.

"Dog no howl?" asked Pemberton.

"No howl," said the Chinese.

Pemberton shrugged his shoulders.

"Shucks," he said, "that's all we need. You can see for yourself, Mason, how it is. Your man just went off his nut, that's all."

"Well," Perry Mason told him, "I'd have asked the questions of this Chinese boy in a little different way."

"That's all right," Pemberton said, "I know how to handle them. Had lots of experience on lottery cases. You've got to talk to them that way. They don't savvy any other kind of lingo. It's the way they talk and the way they learn English. That's the way you get the facts out of them. You go ahead and spout a lot of language they don't understand, and they'll say yes, every time, and not know what they're saying yes to."

"I think," said Mrs. Benton, "that Mr. Foley would like to have you gentlemen wait in the library, if you care to. He'll be with you in just a moment."

She held open the door of the kitchen, and the two men walked through a serving pantry, a dining room, a living room, turned to the left and entered a library, the walls of which were lined with books. There was a huge table running down the center of the room, deep leather chairs, each with a floor lamp by it, and tall windows, with heavy drapes which could be pulled along poles by an ingenious cord arrangement, so as to shut out every bit of outside light.

"I think," said Mrs. Benton, "that if you will just be seated . . ."

A door opened explosively, and Clinton Foley stood on the threshold, his face twisting with emotion, his eyes glittering. A paper was in his hand.

"Well," he said, "it's all over. You don't need to worry about the dog."

The deputy sheriff puffed on his cigar complacently.

"I quit worrying about him as soon as I talked with this girl and the Chink cook," he said. "We're going over and see Cartright now."

Foley laughed, and his laugh was harsh and metallic. At the sound of that laugh, Bill Pemberton took the cigar from his lips, and stared with a perplexed frown.

"Something wrong?" he asked.

"My wife," said Clinton Foley, drawing himself up with some dignity, "has seen fit to run away. She has left with another man."

Pemberton said nothing. Perry Mason stood with feet wide apart, staring from Foley to the young housekeeper, then glancing at Pemberton.

"It may interest you gentlemen to know," said Foley, speaking with the ponderous dignity of one who is trying to conceal his emotions, "that the object of her affections, the man who has supplanted me in her life, is none other than the *gentleman* who lived next door—our esteemed contemporary, Mr. Arthur Cartright, the man who made all of the hullabaloo about the howling dog, in order to get me before the police authorities, so that he could carry out his scheme of running away with my wife."

Perry Mason said in an undertone to Pemberton: "Well, that shows the man isn't crazy; he's crazy like a fox."

Foley came striding into the room, glowering at Perry Mason.

"That will do, sir," he said. "You are here by sufferance only. You will keep your remarks to yourself."

Perry Mason made no move, but with his feet planted apart, shoulders squared, eyes staring in somber appraisal at the man, said slowly: "I'm here to represent my client. You made the accusation that he was crazy and offered to produce evidence. I'm here to see the thing is handled in such a manner that his interests are protected. You can't bluff me a damn bit."

Clinton Foley seemed beside himself. He drew back his right hand, his mouth was twisting and quivering.

Bill Pemberton stepped forward hastily.

"There, there," he said soothingly, "let's not fly off the handle, Foley."

Foley took a deep breath, controlled himself by an effort, just when it seemed he was about to swing his fist at Perry Mason's jaw.

Perry Mason stood perfectly still, not budging so much as an inch.

Foley turned slowly to Pemberton and said in a low, choking voice:

"There's something we can do with swine like that; can't we get out a warrant for his arrest?"

"I think you can," said Pemberton. "But that's up to the district attorney. How do you know she went with him?"

"She says so in this note," said Foley. "Here, read it."

He thrust it into Pemberton's hands, and abruptly turned away, walking to the other end of the room. He lit a cigarette with a hand that trembled, bit his lip, then took a handkerchief from his pocket and blew his nose violently.

Mrs. Benton remained in the room, making no excuses, giving no explanations. Twice she looked long and intently toward Clinton Foley, but Foley had turned his back and was standing at the window, staring out with unseeing eyes.

Perry Mason moved forward and peered over Pemberton's shoulder, as the deputy sheriff unfolded the note. Pemberton shifted so that Mason could not see the note, and Mason good-naturedly put a hand on Pemberton's shoulder, turned him back. "Be a sport," he said.

Pemberton made no further effort to conceal the contents of the letter. Perry Mason read it at the same time Pemberton read it.

The note was in ink and read:

"DEAR CLINTON:

"It is with greatest reluctance that I take the step I am about to take. I know your pride and how much you dislike publicity. I have tried to do this in such a manner that you will be hurt as little as possible. After all, you have been good to me. I thought that I loved you. Up until a few days ago I was absolutely sincere in that belief, then I found out who our next door neighbor was. At first, I was angry, or thought I was angry. He was spying on me with glasses. I should have told you, but something led me to keep it from you. I wanted to see him, and when you were gone I arranged an interview.

"Clinton, there's no use keeping up the pretense any longer. I can't stay with you. I really don't love you; it was just a fascination of the moment—something that has worn itself out.

"You are just a big magnetic animal. You can't overlook a woman, any more than a moth can overlook a flame. I know of the things that have happened right here in the house, and I don't blame you because I don't think you are to blame. I don't think you can help it, but I do know that I don't love you any more. I don't think I ever did. I think it was simply that fascination, that peculiar hypnotic charm which you exercise over women. At any rate, I am going away with him, Clinton.

"I am doing it in such a way that you will be spared any publicity. I am not even telling Thelma Benton where I am going. She only knows that I am taking a suitcase and going away. You can tell her that I have gone to visit some of my relatives, if you wish. If you don't give the affair any publicity, you can rest assured that I will not.

"In your way, you have been good to me. You have gratified my every material wish. The only thing that you can't give me is the love of a true man, nor can you satisfy that hunger in my soul which only he can satisfy. I am going with him, and know that I will be happy.

"Please try to forget me. Believe me,

"Your sincere well wisher,

"EVELYN"

Mason spoke in a low voice.

"She doesn't mention Cartright's name," he said.

"No," Pemberton said, "but she mentions him as being the man next door."

"And," said Perry Mason, in the same low tone, "there's something else about that letter that . . ."

Foley abruptly whirled from the window. The tragic grief which had seemed to affect him so strongly, was gone. There was cold, purposeful rage in his voice and manner.

"Look here," he said, "I'm a wealthy man. I'm willing to give every goddamned cent I've got to have that hound brought to justice. He's crazy, and my wife is crazy. They're both of them crazy. That man's broken up my home; he's accused me of crime; he's tricked me, trapped me, and betrayed me, and, by God, he's going to pay for it! I want you to catch him, and I want him prosecuted on every count you can bring up—violation of ordinances, crossing state lines, or anything else. Spare no expense. I'll pay the bill, no matter what it is."

"Okay," said Bill Pemberton, folding the letter and handing it back to Foley. "I'll go back and make a report. You'd better come back with me. You can talk with Pete Dorcas. Dorcas can figure out some charges to put against this man. Then you can hire some private detective agency, if you want to spend some money."

"I wonder," said Perry Mason, "if there's a telephone here I could use?"

Foley looked at him with cold fury.

47

"You can use the telephone," he said, "and then you can get out."

"Thanks for the invitation," said Perry Mason calmly, "I'll use the telephone anyway."

CHAPTER V

Perry Mason got Della Street on the telephone.

"Mason talking, Della," he said. "I'm out at Clinton Foley's house. He's the one who owns the dog that Cartright was complaining about. Did you get any word from Cartright?"

"No, Chief," she said. "I rang the place every ten minutes for more than an hour, and no one answered."

"All right," he said, "I guess no one's going to answer. It seems that Foley's wife ran off with our client."

"What?" she exclaimed.

"Fact," he told her. "The woman left a note telling Foley all about it. He's furious and is going to arrest Cartright. He and Pemberton are on their way up to the district attorney's office to try and get out a warrant."

"What grounds can they get a warrant on?" asked Della Street. "I thought there could only be a civil action for that."

"Oh, they'll find some crime that they can pin on him," said Perry Mason cheerfully. "It won't be anything that'll hold water, but it'll be enough to save their faces. You see, Cartright evidently used this excuse about the howling dog to decoy Foley away from the house. When Foley went up to the district attorney's office this morning, Cartright skipped out with Foley's wife. Naturally, the district attorney's office won't like that. It will make a funny story for the newspapers."

"Are the newspapers going to get hold of it?" asked Della Street.

"I don't know. I can't tell too much about it right now, but I'm going to work on the case, and I just wanted to let you know that you didn't need to try to get Cartright any more."

"You'll be in the office soon?" she asked.

"I don't know," he said, "it'll be a little while."

"Going to see the district attorney?" she inquired.

"No," he told her, "you can't get me anywhere until I show up or telephone again. But here's something I want you to do. Ring up Drake's Detective Bureau and get Paul Drake to drop anything he's got and come to my office. Have him waiting there when I return. I think it's going to be important as the very devil, so be sure that Drake delegates anything he's working on now, and that he's there in person."

"I'll do that," she said. "Anything else, Chief?"

"That's all," he said. "Be seeing you. 'Bye."

He hung up the receiver, walked from the little closet where the telephone was placed, and encountered the hostile eyes of the housekeeper.

"Mr. Foley said that I was to show you out," she remarked.

"That's all right," Mason told her. "I'm going out, but you might pick up twenty dollars if you wanted to make a little pocket money."

"I don't want to make any pocket money," she said. "My orders were to show you out."

"If," said Perry Mason, "you could find me a photograph of Mrs. Clinton Foley, it might be worth twenty dollars to you. It might even be worth twenty-five dollars."

Her face did not change expression.

"My orders," she said coldly, "were to show you out."

"Well," said Perry Mason, "would you mind telling Mr. Foley on his return that I tried to bribe you to get a picture of his wife?"

"My orders," she said, "were to show you out."

There was the sound of a bell jangling its summons. Mrs. Benton frowned, then looked at Perry Mason, and, for a moment, the mask of her manner dropped from her. There was feminine petulance in her tone.

"Will you *please* leave?" she said.

"Sure," said Perry Mason, "I'm going."

She escorted him to the front door, and, as they walked through the hall, the bell rang twice more.

"Shall I get you a taxicab?" she asked.

"No," said Mason, "don't worry about me."

Abruptly, she turned to him.

"Why," she asked, "are you so anxious to get a picture of Mrs. Foley?"

"Just wanted to see what she looks like," Perry Mason retorted cheerfully.

"No, that wasn't it. You had some reason."

As Mason was about to answer, the bell rang again, and there was the sound of knuckles banging against the wood.

The young woman gave an exclamation of annoyance, and hurried toward the door. As she opened it, three men pushed their way into the hallway.

"Clinton Foley live here?" asked one of the men.

"Yes," said Mrs. Benton.

Perry Mason stepped back into the shadows of the hallway.

"Got a Chinese cook working here, haven't you? Fellow named Ah Wong?"

"Yes."

"All right, get him. We want to see him."

"He's in the kitchen."

"All right, go ahead and get him. Tell him we want to see him."

"But who are you?"

"We're officers—immigration officers. We're checking up on the Chinks. We've got a hot tip he's an illegal entry. Go and get him."

"I'll tell him," she said, and turning on her heel, almost ran past Perry Mason.

The three men, heedless of Mason's presence, walked closely behind her.

After a moment, Perry Mason turned and followed them through the living room, dining room, and into the kitchen. He paused in the serving pantry, and heard the voices of the officers.

"All right, Ah Wong," said one of the men, "where's your certificate? You catchum *chuck jee?*"

"No savvy," said the Chinese.

"Oh, yes, you savvy," said the man. "Where your papers? Where your *chuck jee?* You heap catchum plenty fast."

"Heap no savvy," said the Chinese, with a wail of despair in his voice.

There was a good-natured laugh, the sound of a scuffle, then the man's voice said: "All right, Ah Wong, you come along with us. You show us where you sleep. You show us your things. You savvy? We help you look for *chuck jee.*"

"No savvy, no savvy," wailed the Chinese. "Maybe so you callum somebody make inte'plet whassa malla."

"Forget it and come along."

"No savvy. You catchum inte'pleta."

A man laughed. "He savvies, all right," he said. "Look at his face."

Perry Mason heard the housekeeper's voice raised in protest.

"Can't you wait until Mr. Foley returns? I know that he'll do anything he can for Ah Wong. He's very wealthy, and he'll pay any fine, or put up any bail. . . ."

"Nothing doing, sister," said one of the men. "We've been looking for Ah Wong for a while and there isn't enough money in the mint to keep him here. He's in the laboring class, and he's smuggled in from Mexico. He's headed back for China right now. Come on, Ah Wong, get your things packed."

Perry Mason turned around, tiptoed back the way he had come, and let himself out the front door. He walked down the stairs from the porch to the sidewalk, walked briskly along the sidewalk until he came to the house on the north, where Arthur Cartright lived. He turned in at the cement walk which ran across a well-kept lawn, ran up the steps, to the front porch, and pressed his thumb against the button of the doorbell. He could hear the bell jangling from the interior of the house, but could hear no sounds of motion. He pounded on the panels of the door with his knuckles, and received no answer. He moved along the porch until he came to a window, and tried to peer in the window, but the curtains were drawn. He returned to the door and rang the bell.

There were faint sounds of motion from the interior of the house, then shuffling steps, and a curtain was pulled back from a small, circular window in the center of the door. A thin, tired face peered out at him, while weary, emotionless eyes studied him.

After an interval, a lock clicked back, and the door opened.

Perry Mason was facing a gaunt woman of fifty-five, with faded hair, eyes that seemed to have been bleached of color, a thin, determined mouth, a pointed jaw and long, straight nose.

"What do you want?" she asked, in the even monotone of one who is deaf.

"I want Mr. Cartright," said Perry Mason in a loud voice.

"I can't hear you; you'll have to speak a little louder."

"I want Mr. Cartright, Mr. Arthur Cartright," Mason shouted.

"He isn't here."

"Where is he?"

"I don't know; he isn't here."

Perry Mason took a step toward her, placed his mouth close to her ear.

"Look here," he said, "I'm Mr. Cartright's lawyer. I've got to see him at once."

She stepped back and studied him with her weary, faded eyes, then slowly shook her head.

"I heard him speak of you," she said. "I knew he had a lawyer. He wrote you a letter last night, then he went away. He gave me the letter to mail, did you get it all right?"

Mason nodded.

"What's your name?" she asked.

"Perry Mason," he shouted.

"That's right," she said. "That's the name that was on the envelope."

Her face was entirely placid, without so much as the faintest flicker of an expression. Her voice maintained the same even monotone.

Perry Mason moved toward her once more, placed his lips close to her ear, and yelled: "When did Mr. Cartright go out?"

"Last night about half past ten."

"Did he come back after that?"

"No."

"Did he take a suitcase with him?"

"No."

"Had he been packing any of his things?"

"No, he burned some letters."

"Acted as though he was getting ready to go away somewhere?"

"He burned letters and papers, that's all I know."

"Did he say where he was going when he went out?"

"No."

"Did he have a car?"

"No, he hasn't a car."

"Did he order a taxicab?"

"No, he walked."

"You didn't see where he went?"

"No, it was dark."

"Do you mind if I come in?"

"It won't do you any good to come in. Mr. Cartright isn't here."

"Do you mind if I come in and wait until he comes back?"

"He's been out all night. I don't know that he's going to come back."

"Did he tell you he wasn't coming back?"

"No."

"Are your wages paid?"

"That's none of your business."

"I'm his lawyer."

"It's still none of your business."

"You don't know what was in the letter you were given to mail to me last night?"

"No, that's none of my business. You mind your business and I'll mind mine."

"Look here," said Perry Mason, "this is important. I want you to go through the house and see if you can find anything that will help me. I've got to find Arthur Cartright. If he's gone somewhere, I've got to find where he's gone. You've got to find something that will give me a clew. I want to know whether he went by train, whether he went by automobile or whether he went by airplane. He must have made some reservations, or done something."

"I don't know," said the woman. "That's none of my business. I clean up the house for him, that's all. I'm deaf. I can't hear things that go on."

"What's your name?" asked Perry Mason.

"Elizabeth Walker."

"How long have you known Mr. Cartright?"

"Two months."

"Do you know anything about his friends? Do you know anything about his family?"

"I know nothing except about keeping the house."

"Will you be here later on?"

"Of course I'll be here. I'm supposed to stay here. That's what I'm paid for."

"How long will you stay if Mr. Cartright doesn't return?"

"I'll stay until my time's up."

"When will that be?"

"That," she said, "is my business, Mr. Lawyer. Good-by." She slammed the door with a force which shook the house.

Perry Mason stood staring at the door for a moment, with a half smile on his face. Then he turned and walked down the steps from the porch. As he reached the sidewalk, he felt the peculiar tingling sensation of the hairs at the base of his neck which caused him to whirl suddenly and stare.

He was in time to see heavy drapes slip back into place over a window in the house of Clinton Foley. He could not see the face that had been staring at him from that window.

CHAPTER VI

PAUL DRAKE was a tall man with drooping shoulders, a head that was thrust forward, eyes that held an expression of droll humor. Long experience with the vagaries of human nature had made him take everything, from murder down, with a serene tranquillity.

He was waiting in Perry Mason's office, when Mason returned.

Perry Mason smiled at Della Street, and said to the detective: "Come right in, Paul."

Drake followed him into the inner office.

"What's it all about?"

"I'll give it to you short and snappy," said Mason. "A man named Cartright, living at 4893 Milpas Drive, complains that a chap named Clinton Foley, living at 4889 Milpas Drive, has a dog that howls. Cartright is nervous, perhaps a little bit unbalanced. I take him to Pete Dorcas to get a complaint and arrange to have Dr. Charles Cooper look him over. Cooper diagnoses it as manic depressive psychosis; nothing serious. That is, it's functional, rather than organic. I insist that the continued howling of a dog can be very serious to a man of such nervous instability. Dorcas writes Foley a summons to appear and show cause why a warrant shouldn't be issued.

"Foley gets the summons, shows up at the district attorney's office this morning, and I go over. Foley claims the dog hasn't been howling. Dorcas is ready to commit Cartright as insane. I put up a fight, and claim Foley's lying about the dog. He offers to take us to witnesses to prove the dog didn't howl. We go out to his house. His wife has been sick in bed. He's got a housekeeper who's a good-looking Jane, but tries to make herself look older than she is, and uglier. The dog is a police dog they've had for about a year. The housekeeper reports somebody poisoned the dog early in the morning. She gave him a bunch of salt, got him to throw up the poison, and saved his life. The dog, apparently, was having spasms. He bit her on the right hand and arm. She's wearing a bandage that looks as though a physician had put it on, so it seems the bite was pretty serious, or else she was afraid the dog was mad. She says the dog hasn't been howling. The Chink cook says the dog hasn't been howling.

"Foley goes to talk with his wife, and finds she's gone. The housekeeper says she left a note. Foley gets the note, and it's a note telling him that she doesn't really love him; that it was just one of those fatal fascinations, and all that line of hooey a woman springs when she's falling out of love with some man, and into love with another. She says that she's leaving with the man next door, and that she really loves *him*."

Drake's expression of droll humor broadened into a grin.

"You mean she ran away with the crazy guy next door that thought the dog was howling?"

"That seems to be the sketch. Foley claims Cartright made up the complaint about the howling dog out of whole cloth and worked it as a scheme to get him away from his house so that Cartright would have a clear field to walk away with Mrs. Foley."

Drake chuckled.

"And Foley still claims Cartright's crazy!" he exclaimed.

Perry Mason grinned.

"Well," he said, "he wasn't claiming the man was crazy quite so strong when I left."

"How did it affect him?" asked the detective.

"That's the funny thing," said Mason. "I'd swear he was putting it on too thick. He either wasn't as broken up as he pretended to be, or else there was something that he was trying to cover up. I think he's had an affair with his housekeeper. I think the wife intimated as much in the note. At any rate, he's been playing around. He's one of these big, dominant men with a vibrant voice and a strong personality. He's got a great deal of poise, and seemed to have quite a bit of control over his temper. He was magnanimous and broad-minded when he was up in the district attorney's office, trying to get Cartright committed. He claimed that he wanted to do it only because he thought Cartright needed treatment. He said that he'd put up with a lot of espionage before making a complaint.

"Now, a man of that type wouldn't fly off the handle the way he did, under ordinary circumstances, when he found that his wife was gone—not a man of his type. He isn't a one-woman man. He's the kind who plays the field."

"Maybe it's something about Cartright that he hates," Drake suggested.

"That's exactly the point that I'm coming to," the lawyer told him. "The woman's note indicated that she had known Cartright and had been acquainted with him. Cartright moved into the house about two months ago. Foley has been in his place for about a year, and there's some stuff about it I can't understand.

"It's a big place and in an exclusive neighborhood. Foley must have money; yet he and his wife were getting along with just a cook and a housekeeper. Apparently there was no butler, valet or chauffeur. I think you'll find they didn't do any entertaining at all. Ordinarily, I would have said the house was far too big for them, but not only are they living in it, without a chauffeur, but Foley is having an addition built onto the garage. It's of reënforced concrete, and the thing is being finished up this morning. They've poured the floor, and the rest of the building is finished."

"Well, what's wrong with that?" asked Drake. "He's got a right to build an addition onto his garage, hasn't he?"

"But what does he want it for?" asked Mason. "The garage is big enough to hold three cars. Foley has got two cars in there, and he doesn't keep a chauffeur."

"Perhaps he wanted to get a car for his housekeeper," said Drake, grinning.

"Perhaps," Mason admitted. "Or he may want separate quarters."

"No use speculating," Drake said. "Where do I come in?"

"I want you," said Mason, "to find out everything you can about Foley——where he came from and why; also the same thing about Cartright. I want you to put just as many men to work as you can use to advantage. I want the information, and I want it fast, and I want it in advance of the police, if I can get it.

"I think you'll find there's something fishy about this whole business. I think you'll find that Cartright knows Foley, or has known him sometime in the past, and that he came to the neighborhood, rented the house that he

58

did, for the deliberate purpose of spying on Foley. I want to know why."

Paul Drake stroked his chin meditatively, then let his eyes casually drift to the lawyer's face.

"Come clean," he said. "What's the lowdown?"

"I've given you the lowdown, Paul."

"Oh, no, you haven't, Perry. You're representing a client who complained about a howling dog. The client has gone by-by with a married woman. Apparently she's a good looking married woman. Everybody's happy except the outraged husband. He's gone up to the district attorney's office. You know that he isn't going to get very much out of the district attorney except a song and dance. There's no reason for you to get so worked up about this thing, unless there's something that you haven't told me about."

"Well," said Mason slowly, "I think I may be representing more than one person. I haven't stopped to figure exactly the professional ethics of the situation, but there's a chance I may be representing Mrs. Foley, as well."

"Well," said Drake, grinning, "she's happy, isn't she?"

"I don't know," said Perry Mason, his eyes narrowing. "I want to get all of the dope that I can on the entire situation, and I want to find out just who these people are, and where they came from."

"Got any photographs?" asked Drake.

"No, I haven't. I tried to get some, but couldn't get them. There's a deaf housekeeper out at Cartright's place, and I told you the hook-up on the housekeeper at Foley's place. I tried to bribe her to get some pictures, and didn't get anywhere with it. She'll tell Foley, that's a cinch. Apparently she's loyal to him. Here's another funny thing: just before I left, immigration officers came and picked up the Chink cook for deportation, on the ground that he didn't have a certificate, and I guess he didn't. He's a Chinese of around forty or forty-five, and unless he's native born, he's probably headed for China."

"Will Foley put up a fight for him?"

"The girl said he would," Mason answered.

"What girl?"

"The housekeeper."

"Girl, eh?"

"Well, she's a young woman."

"You seem to think she's got plenty of IT."

"She's got something," said Mason slowly, "and I don't know what it is. She's gone to a lot of trouble to make herself up so she looks plain and homely. Women don't ordinarily do that."

Paul Drake grinned slowly.

"Women ordinarily do anything they damned please," he said.

Perry Mason said nothing for a few minutes, but drummed silently with his fingertips on the surface of the desk. Then he looked over at Paul Drake.

"The housekeeper says that Mrs. Foley left there in a taxicab this morning. Now, Cartright left his place last night and didn't come back. He was in very much of a hurry, because he sent an important letter to me by special delivery, but had his housekeeper mail it. Now, if you can find the taxicab that called for Mrs. Foley, and find where she was taken, you're quite likely to find some trace of Cartright at that place. That is, if the housekeeper is telling the truth."

"You think she isn't?"

"I don't know. I want to get all of the facts, then I'll sift them and sort them. I want the most complete reports possible. Put enough men on it to familiarize yourself with every angle of the case. Find out who these people are, where they've been, what they're doing and why."

"Put a tail on Foley?"

"Yes, put a tail on Foley. But don't let him know it. I want him watched wherever he goes."

Paul Drake got to his feet and ambled in a leisurely way toward the door.

"I get you," he said, "I'll get started."

He opened the door, stepped through the outer office and vanished.

Apparently the man moved with a shambling, leisurely stride; yet an ordinary man would have been hard put to keep up with him. Paul Drake's efficiency, both in his work and in his motions, lay in the fact that he never became excited and never wasted time in lost motion.

When the detective had gone, Perry Mason summoned Della Street into his office.

"Della," he said, "cancel every appointment that I've got. Hold everything wide open. Clear the decks for action."

She let her shrewd hazel eyes study him in calm appraisal.

"You know something?" she asked.

"Nothing much," he told her. "It's just a hunch. I think something's going to break."

"You mean in that Cartright case?"

He nodded.

"How about the money? Do you want that put in the bank?"

He nodded again. He arose from his chair and started pacing the office, with the restless stride of a lion pacing a cage.

"What is it?" she asked. "What's wrong?"

"I don't know," he told her, "but things don't click."

"How do you mean they don't click?"

"They don't fit together. They look all right on the surface, except for a loose joint or two, but those loose joints are significant. There's something wrong."

"Have you any idea what it is?"

"Not yet, but I'm going to have."

She walked toward the outer office, paused in the door to flash him a solicitous glance. Her eyes were warm with affection.

He was pacing the floor back and forth, thumbs thrust

in the armholes of his vest, head forward, eyes staring intently at the carpet.

CHAPTER VII

IT WAS ten minutes before five when Perry Mason called Pete Dorcas on the telephone.

"Perry Mason talking, Pete. How do I stand with you?"

"Not very high," said Dorcas, but there was a trace of humor in his rasping, querulous voice. "You're too damned belligerent. Any time a fellow tries to do you a favor, he gets into trouble. You get too enthusiastic over your clients."

"I wasn't enthusiastic," said Mason; "I simply claimed the man wasn't crazy."

Dorcas laughed.

"Well," he said, "you're sure right on that. The man wasn't crazy. He played things pretty foxy."

"What are you doing about it; anything?"

"No. Foley came in here all steamed up. He wanted to get warrants issued right and left; wanted to turn the universe upside down, and then he wasn't so certain that he wanted the publicity. He asked me to wait until he communicated with me again."

"Well, did you hear from him later?"

"Yes, about ten minutes ago."

"What did he say?"

"Said that his wife had sent him a telegram from some little town down the state—Midwick, I think it was, begging him not to do anything that would bring about a lot of newspaper publicity. She said it wouldn't do him any good, and would do them all a lot of harm."

"What did you do?"

"Oh, the usual thing. I pigeonholed it. It's nothing except a man's wife running off with somebody else. They're free, white and twenty-one, and know what they're doing. Of course, if they set up a meretricious relationship, openly and defiantly in some community, that will be a problem for that community to handle, but we can't spend a lot of time and money bringing some fellow's wife back to him when she doesn't want to come.

"Of course, he's got a good civil action against your client, Cartright, and the way Foley was talking this morning, he was going to file actions for alienation of affections, and everything else he could think of, but I have an idea he's changing his mind on that."

"Well," Mason told him, "I just wanted you to know the way I felt about it. I gave you a fair deal right from the start. I gave you a chance to have a doctor there to look Cartright over."

"Well, the man isn't crazy, that's a cinch," Dorcas said. "I'll buy you a cigar the next time I see you."

"No, I'm going to buy you the cigars," Mason told him. "In fact, I'm having a box sent over right now. How long you going to be at the office?"

"About fifteen minutes."

"Stick around," said Mason, "the cigars will be there."

He hung up the telephone, went to the door of his outer office and said to Della Street: "Ring up the cigar stand across the street from the Hall of Justice. Tell them to take a box of fifty-cent cigars up to Pete Dorcas, and charge them to me. I think he's got them coming."

"Yes, sir," she said. "Mr. Drake telephoned while you were talking on the line to Dorcas. He says he's got something for you, and I told him to come up, that you'd be anxious to see him."

"Where was he, down in his office?"

"Yes."

"All right," said Mason, "when he comes, send him right in."

He walked back to his desk and had no sooner sat down than the door opened, and Paul Drake walked into the room with that same ungainly stride which masked such efficiency of motion as to make his advance seem unhurried, yet he was seated in a chair across from the lawyer, with a cigarette going, before the door check had closed the door.

"Well," said Mason, "what have you found out?"

"Lots of stuff."

"All right, go ahead and tell me."

Drake pulled a notebook from his pocket.

"Is it so much you can't tell me without a notebook?" asked Mason.

"It sure is, and it's cost you a lot of money."

"I don't care about that, I wanted the information."

"Well, we got it. We had to burn up the wires and get a couple of affiliated agencies working on the case."

"Never mind that; give me the dope."

"She isn't his wife," said Paul Drake.

"Who isn't?"

"The woman who lived with Foley at 4889 Milpas Drive, and went under the name of Evelyn Foley."

"Well," said Mason, "that's no great shock to me. To tell you the truth, Paul, that's one of the reasons I wanted you to work on the case. I had an idea that she wasn't."

"How did you get that idea? From something Cartright told you?" asked the detective.

"You tell me what you know first," said Mason.

"Well," said Drake, "the woman's name wasn't Evelyn. That's her middle name. Her first name was Paula. Her full name is Paula Evelyn Cartright. She's the wife of your client, Arthur Cartright."

Perry Mason slowly nodded.

"You haven't surprised me yet, Paul," he said.

"Well, I probably won't surprise you with anything, then," said Drake, thumbing the pages of his notebook. "Here's the dope: Clinton Foley's real name is Clinton Forbes. He and his wife, Bessie Forbes, lived in Santa Barbara. They were friendly with Arthur Cartright and Paula Cartright. The friendship between Forbes and Mrs. Cartright ripened into an intimacy, and they ran away together. Neither Bessie Forbes nor Arthur Cartright knew where the others had gone. It was quite a scandal in Santa Barbara. The people mingled with the better class of society there, and you can imagine what a choice bit of scandal it made. Forbes was independently wealthy, and he translated all of his belongings into cash so that he could carry it with him, without leaving any back trail. They left by automobile, and left no clews as to where they were going.

"Cartright, however, managed to find them. I don't know how he did it. He traced Forbes, and found that Clinton Foley was, in reality, Clinton Forbes, and that the woman who went under the name of Evelyn Foley was, in reality, Paula Cartright, his wife."

"Then," said Perry Mason slowly, "why did Cartright get the adjoining house and spy on Foley, or Forbes, whichever you want to call him?"

"What the devil could he do?" asked Drake. "The woman left of her own free will. She ran away from him. He couldn't have gone over and said: 'Here I am, sweetheart,' and have her fall into his arms."

"You haven't got the idea yet," Mason said.

Drake looked at him for a moment, and then said: "You mean he was plotting revenge?"

"Yes," Mason said.

"Well," the detective drawled, "when he finally got around to springing his plan for revenge, it didn't amount to anything more than complaining about the howling of a dog. That's not much of a revenge. You've heard the story about the irate husband who cut holes in the umbrella of a man who was entertaining his wife."

"Wait a minute," Mason said. "I'm not joking; I'm serious."

"Well, all right," Drake remarked. "Suppose you *are* serious? What does that buy us?"

"The theory of the district attorney's office is that Cartright complained about the howling dog merely in order to get Foley away from home, so Cartright could run off with Foley's wife."

"Well?" asked the detective.

"It doesn't make sense," the lawyer said. "In the first place, why go to all that elaborate trouble in order to get Foley away from home? In the second place, there must have been some previous talks between Cartright and his wife. He must have known where she was, and she must have known where he was. Those talks necessarily took place in the absence of Foley. Having decided that they were going to go back together and patch things up, why the devil didn't Cartright walk over to the place, cuss Foley out and take his wife?"

"Probably because he didn't have the guts," Drake said. "There are people like that."

"All right," Mason agreed patiently, "let's suppose you're right on that. Then he went to the law, didn't he?"

"Yes."

"How much simpler it would have been to go to the law and complain that Foley was living in a meretricious relationship with his wife, and have the law step in. Or, he could have hired me as his attorney, and I'd have gone out there and pulled the woman out of the house damned quick. That is, if she wanted to get away. Or, the woman could simply have walked out. After all, Cartright had all of the legal rights on his side."

Drake shook his head.

"Well," he said, "that's up to you. What you wanted me to do was to get the facts. You were going to put them together."

Mason nodded slowly.

"What do you think happened?" asked Drake.

"I don't know," Mason said, "but I'm telling you that the thing doesn't click. It doesn't fit together and it doesn't make sense, and the farther we go into it, the less sense it makes."

"Now, then," Drake said, "who are you representing?"

"I'm not entirely certain," Mason said slowly. "I'm representing Arthur Cartright, and I may be representing his wife, or I may be representing Foley's wife. By the way, what happened to her?"

"You mean Forbes?" asked the detective.

"Foley or Forbes, it's all the same. I know him as Foley; that's the way I first met him, so that's the way I describe him."

"Well," said Drake, "we haven't had any luck on tracing Mrs. Forbes yet. Naturally, she felt quite a bit disgraced and she left Santa Barbara, but we don't know where she went. You know how a woman would feel about those things, particularly when a man didn't give her any warning, but simply disappeared and took a friend's wife with him."

Mason nodded slowly, and reached for his hat.

"I think," he said, "that I'm going out and talk with this Clinton Forbes, alias Clinton Foley."

"Well," Drake told him, "every man to his taste. You may have your hands full. He's got the reputation for being a belligerent customer, and having the devil's own temper. I found that out in checking back on his career in Santa Barbara."

Mason nodded absently.

"That's one thing they can't ever say about you," Drake remarked. "They can't ever say you haven't got guts. You go out of your way in order to get into trouble."

Perry Mason shook his head, paused for a moment, then walked back to his desk, sat down and picked up the telephone.

"Della," he said, "get me Clinton Foley on the line. His residence is 4889 Milpas Drive. I want to talk with him personally."

"What's the idea?" asked Drake.

"I'm going to make an appointment with him. I'm not going to chase all the way out there, only to find that I've run up a taxi bill."

"If he knows you're coming, he'll have a couple of bouncers waiting to throw you out," the detective warned.

"Not after I get done talking with him, he won't," Mason said grimly.

Paul Drake sighed and lit a cigarette.

"A fool for a fight," he said.

"No, I'm not," Mason told him. "But you overlook the fact that I'm representing my clients. I'm a paid gladiator. I have to go in and fight; that's what they hire me for. Any time I get weak-kneed so I don't have guts enough to wade in and fight, I've unfitted myself to carry on my profession, at any rate, the branch of it that I specialize in. I'm a fighter. I'm hired to fight. Everything I got in the world, I got through fighting."

The telephone rang, and Mason scooped up the receiver.

"Mr. Foley on the line," Della Street's voice said.

"Okay," Mason told her.

There was the click of the connection, and then Foley's voice, vibrant with booming magnetism.

"Yes, hello, hello."

"Mr. Foley," said the lawyer, "this is Perry Mason, the attorney. I want to talk with you."

"I have nothing whatever to discuss with you, Mr. Mason," Foley said.

"I wanted to talk with you about the affairs of a client who lived in Santa Barbara," said Perry Mason.

There was a moment of silence. The buzzing noise of the wire was all that could be heard. Then Foley's voice came, pitched a note lower.

"And what was the name of this client?" he asked.

"Well," Mason told him, "we might agree on a tentative name of Forbes."

"Man or woman?" asked Foley.

"A woman—a married woman. Her husband had run off and left her."

"And what did you want to see *me* about?" Foley demanded.

"I'll explain that to you when I see you."

"Very well, when will you see me?"

"As soon as convenient."

"Tonight at eight-thirty?"

"Can you make it any earlier?"

"No."

"Very well, I will be at your place at nine o'clock tonight," said Mason, and slid the receiver back on the hook.

Paul Drake shook his head lugubriously.

"You do take the damnedest chances," he said. "You'd better have me go out there with you."

"No," Mason told him, "I'm going out there alone."

"All right," the detective said, "let me give you a tip, then. You'd better go prepared for trouble. That man's in a dangerous mood."

"What do you mean prepared for trouble?"

"Carry a gun," the detective said.

Perry Mason shook his head.

"I carry my two fists," he said, "and my wits. I fight with those. Sometimes I carry a gun, but I don't make a practice of it. It's bad training. It teaches one to rely entirely on a gun. Force should only be a last resort."

"Have it your own way," Drake remarked.

"How about the housekeeper?" said Mason. "You haven't told me about her yet."

"The housekeeper didn't change her name."

"You mean she was with Forbes before he became Foley?"

"That's right. Her name is Mrs. Thelma Benton. Her husband was killed in an automobile accident. She was employed as a private secretary to Forbes when he was in Santa Barbara. She accompanied him on his trip. But here's the funny thing: apparently Mrs. Cartright didn't know that Thelma Benton had been employed by Forbes as a secretary. The young woman came with them as a housekeeper, and Mrs. Cartright never knew she'd been Forbes' secretary."

"That's strange, isn't it?"

"Not particularly. You see, Forbes had an office in Santa Barbara where he transacted his business. Naturally he was rather secretive about it, because he was getting his affairs turned into cash. Evidently the secretary suspected a good deal, and he didn't want to leave her behind, or she didn't want to be left behind, I don't know which. She went with them when they left."

"How about the Chinese cook?"

"He's a new addition. They picked him up here."

Perry Mason shrugged his broad shoulders.

"The whole thing sounds goofy," he said. "I'll tell you a lot more about it tonight, however. You'd better be in your office, Paul, so I can call you if I want any information."

"Okay," Drake told him, "and I don't mind telling you that I'm going to have men outside, watching the house. You know, we've got a tail on Foley, and I'm just going to double it, so that if there's any trouble, all you've got to do is to kick out a window, or something, and the men will come in."

Perry Mason shook his head with the impatient gesture of a prizefighter shaking hair from in front of his eyes.

"Hell!" he said. "There isn't going to be any trouble."

CHAPTER VIII

THE big house silhouetted itself against the star-studded sky. There was a wind blowing from the south, with a hint of dampness, giving promise of a cloudiness later on in the evening.

Perry Mason looked at the luminous dial of his wristwatch. It was exactly eight-thirty.

He glanced behind him to see the tail light of the taxicab vanishing around a corner. He saw no trace of any watchers who were on duty. With steady, purposeful steps, he climbed the stairs from the cement walk to the porch, and walked to the front door of the house.

It was ajar.

Perry Mason found the doorbell, pressed his thumb against it.

There was no answer.

He waited a moment, then rang again, with the same result.

Perry Mason looked at his watch, frowned impatiently, took a few steps along the porch, paused, came back, and pounded on the door. There was still no answer.

Perry Mason stepped to the door, looked down the corridor and saw a light coming from the door of the library. He pushed his way down the corridor and knocked on the library door.

There was no answer.

He turned the knob and shoved the door open.

The door moved some eighteen inches, then struck against something—an object which was heavy, yet yielding.

Perry Mason eased through the opening in the door, stared at the object which had blocked the door. It was a police dog, lying on his side, with a bullet hole in his chest and another in his head. Blood had trickled from the bullet wounds, along the floor, and when Mason had pushed the door open, moving the body, the stains had smeared over the hardwood floor.

Mason raised his head and looked around the library. At first he saw nothing. Then, at the far end of the room, he saw a blotch of shadow, from which protruded something grayish, which proved, on closer inspection, to be the clutching hand of a man.

Perry Mason walked around the table and switched on one of the floor lamps so that he could see into the corner.

Clinton Foley was stretched at full length on the floor.

One arm was outstretched, the hand clutched tightly. The other hand was doubled under the body.

The man wore a dressing gown of brown flannel, and had slippers on his bare feet. From the body was seeping a pool of red which reflected the floor lamp from its viscid surface.

Perry Mason did not touch the body. He leaned forward and saw that there was an athletic undershirt showing beneath the bathrobe, where it had fallen open at the neck.

He noticed, also, an automatic lying on the floor some six or eight feet from the body.

He turned back to look at the dead man, and saw then that there was something white showing on his chin. He bent forward and observed that it was a spot of caked lather. Part of the right side of the face had been freshly shaven. The evidences of the razor strokes were plainly visible.

Perry Mason walked to the telephone from which he had called his office on the occasion of his prior visit, and dialed the number of Paul Drake's office. After a moment, he heard Paul Drake's drawling voice on the telephone.

"Mason talking, Paul," said Perry Mason. "I'm out here at Foley's house. Can you get in touch with the men you have watching the house out here?"

"They're going to call in in five minutes," said Drake. "I'm having them make reports every fifteen minutes. There are two men on the job. One of them goes to the telephone every fifteen minutes."

"All right," Perry Mason said, "as soon as those men telephone, get them to come to your office at once."

"Both of them?" asked Paul Drake.

"Both of them," Mason said.

"What's the big idea?" asked Drake.

"I'll come to that in a minute," said Mason. "I want both of those men off the job and called into your office where I can talk with them. Do you get that?"

"Okay," Drake said, "I've got that. Anything else?"

"Yes. I want you to double your efforts to find Cartright and Mrs. Cartright."

"I've a couple of agencies working on that now. I'm expecting a report almost any minute."

"All right, get two more agencies working on it. Put up a reward. Anything you can. Now, here's something else."

"Okay," Drake said, "shoot."

"I want you to find Mrs. Forbes."

"You mean the wife that was left behind in Santa Barbara?"

"Yes."

"I think I'm getting a line on her, Perry. I've had some reports that look hot. I think she's going to be turned up almost any minute. I've got men working on some live leads there."

"All right, put on more men. Do anything you can."

"I get you," drawled Drake. "Now tell me what's happened. What's the idea of all the commotion? You had your appointment with Foley at eight thirty. It's now eight thirty-eight, and you say you're telephoning from his house. Did you reach some understanding with him?"

"No."

"Well," said Drake, "what happened?"

"I think," Mason told him, "it will be better if you don't know anything about that until you've followed out my instructions."

"Okay," Drake said. "When will I see you?"

"I don't know. I've got some formalities to go through with. It may be some little time before you see me. But get the men who are watching the house, and keep them under cover. Lock them in your office, if you have to. Don't let any one interview them until I get there. Do you understand that?"

"Okay. I wish you'd tell me what it's all about."

"You'll find out later, but keep those men sewed up tight."

"I'll have 'em on ice," Drake promised.

Perry Mason hung up the 'phone, then dialed the number of police headquarters.

A bored masculine voice answered.

"Police headquarters?" asked Mason.

"Yes."

"All right, get this and get it straight.

"This is Perry Mason, attorney at law. I am talking from the house of Clinton Foley at 4889 Milpas Drive. I had an appointment with Mr. Foley at eight thirty this evening. I came to the house, and found the door ajar. I repeatedly rang the bell and no one answered. I walked into the corridor, came to the library and found Clinton Foley dead. He's been shot twice, or perhaps more than that, with an automatic, at close range."

The voice came over the wire with sudden crisp interest.

"What's that number—4889 Milpas Drive?"

"That's right."

"And what's your name?"

"Perry Mason."

"Perry Mason, the lawyer?"

"That's right."

"Who's with you, anybody?"

"No."

"Who else is in the house?"

"No one that I know of."

"Well, then, stay right there. Don't touch anything. Don't let any one in. If there's any one else in the house, make them stay there. We're sending the Homicide Squad right out."

Perry Mason hung up the telephone, reached for a cigarette, thought better of it, put the case back in his pocket and walked back into the library. He made a hurried search of the library, then pushed his way through a door which opened from the rear of the library. He found that it opened into a bedroom. There was a light burning in the bedroom, and a suit of evening clothes was laid out on the bed.

Mason walked across the room and into a bathroom. On a shelf above the washbowl in the bathroom was a safety razor, shaving cream and a brush, to which lather still clung. The safety razor had been used.

Around a water pipe, leading to the bathtub, was a dog chain, and near the dog chain was a pan of water. On the other side was another pan which was empty. Perry Mason knelt and looked at that empty pan. The bottom of it was smeared with a greasy substance, and around the edges of the pan there were two or three particles of what appeared to be a canned dog food.

The far end of the chain terminated in a spring catch, so devised that a person need only press the prongs of the catch together, to spread the jaws and liberate a dog who might be chained to it.

Mason walked back to the library, ignored the corpse of the man, went to the body of the police dog. There was a collar around the neck, a collar which was shiny with age, and which bore a silver plate. On the silver plate, the words, "PRINCE. PROPERTY OF CLINTON FOLEY. 4889 MILPAS DRIVE," had been engraved. There was also a ring in the collar, in which the jaws of the spring catch on the end of the dog chain in the bathroom would have fitted.

Mason was careful to touch nothing, but moved about the room cautiously. He went back to the bedroom, through the bedroom to the bathroom, and made a second inspection.

Underneath the bathtub, he caught sight of a towel. He pulled out the towel, and noticed that it was still damp. He raised the towel to his nostrils, smelled it, and caught the odor of shaving cream.

As he straightened and pushed the towel back into the position where he had found it, he heard the sound of a siren in the distance, and the noise made by the exhaust of a police car.

Perry Mason walked through the library, into the corridor, noticing, as he did so, that there was barely room for him to squeeze through the door, without moving the body of the dog still further along the hardwood floor.

He walked along the corridor to the front door, and met the officers as they came pounding up on the porch.

CHAPTER IX

BRIGHT incandescents beat pitilessly down upon Perry Mason's face.

On his right, seated at a little table, a shorthand reporter took down everything Mason said.

Across from Mason, Detective Sergeant Holcomb stared at Mason, with eyes that showed a combination of puzzled bewilderment, and a vast irritation. Seated around in the shadows were three men of the homicide squad.

"You don't need to pull all that hokum," said Perry Mason.

"What hokum?" Sergeant Holcomb asked.

"All this business of the bright lights, and all of that. You aren't confusing me any."

Sergeant Holcomb took a deep breath.

"Mason," he said, "there's something about this that you're holding back. Now, we want to know what it is. A murder's been committed, and you're found prowling around the place."

"In other words, you think I shot him, is that it?" Mason countered.

"We don't know what to think," Holcomb said irritably. "We do know that you represented a client who gave every indication of showing incipient homicidal mania. We know that you occupied an adverse position all the way along the line to Clinton Foley, the murdered man. We don't know what you were doing out there. We don't know how you got in the house. We don't know just who it is you're trying to shield, but you're sure as hell trying to shield somebody."

"Maybe I'm trying to shield myself," Perry Mason remarked.

"I'm commencing to think so," Holcomb said.

"That," said Perry Mason, in a tone of finality, "shows just exactly how good a detective you are. If you'd use your brains, you'd realize that the mere fact I am a lawyer representing interests inimical to Clinton Foley would have made him very careful what he said and what he did. His manner toward me would have been one of extreme formality. I'd hardly be a friend that he'd receive in the informality of a bathrobe, with a face that was half shaven."

"Whoever did that job," Sergeant Holcomb said, "broke into the house. The first thing that happened was when the dog heard the intruder. Naturally, the dog would have ears that were more keen than those of his master. His master let the dog loose, and you had to shoot the dog in self-defense. At the sound of those shots, Clinton Foley came running into the room to see what was the matter, and you let him have it."

"You're satisfied of that?" asked Perry Mason.

"It's commencing to look that way."

"Then why don't you arrest me?"

"By God, I'm going to if you don't come clean on this thing! I never in my life ran onto a man in a murder case who was so delightfully indefinite. You say you had an appointment with Foley at eight-thirty. But you don't produce any evidence to prove it."

"What sort of evidence could I produce?"

"Didn't any one hear you make the appointment?"

"I can't remember, I'm sure. I didn't pay very much attention to it when I made it. I just made it in a casual way."

"How about the taxicab that took you out there?"

"I tell you it was a cruising cab. I don't remember what kind it was."

"You haven't got the cab receipt?"

"Certainly not. I don't go around saving receipts from taxi meters."

"What did you do with it? Drop it on the sidewalk?"

"I don't know as I ever saw it."

"You don't remember what sort of a cab you went out in? Whether it was a yellow, a checker, or a red top?"

"Hell, no! I tell you I don't remember all those details. I don't figure that I'm going to be cross-examined on everything I do. I'll tell you something else, too. As a detective, you're a false alarm. The way you reconstruct the scene of that murder shows that you don't know what happened."

"Ah," said Sergeant Holcomb, in the purring tone of one who is about to betray another into a damaging admission, "then you *know* what happened, do you?"

"I looked around," said Perry Mason, "the same as you did."

"Very well," Sergeant Holcomb said sarcastically, "go ahead and tell me what happened, if you will be so good."

"In the first place," said Perry Mason, "the dog was chained up when the murderer went into the house. Clinton Foley went out and saw the person who had entered the house, and talked with him for a minute. Then he went back and turned the dog loose. That was when the dog was shot, and after that Clinton Foley was shot."

"What makes you say all of that?" asked Sergeant Holcomb. "You seem quite positive."

"Did you," asked Perry Mason with scathing sarcasm, "happen to notice a towel lying partially under the bathtub?"

Sergeant Holcomb hesitated for a moment, then said, "What of it?"

"On that towel," said Perry Mason, "was shaving cream."

"Well, what of that?"

"The towel was dropped there when Clinton Foley released the dog from the chain. Now, when a man shaves, he doesn't put shaving cream on a towel. He only gets shaving cream on a towel when he is wiping the lather from his face. He does that hastily, when he is interrupted in the middle of his shaving and wants to clean the surplus lather from his face. Now, Clinton Foley didn't do that when the dog first barked or when he first heard the intruder. He went into the other room to see what the dog was barking about, and faced an intruder. He talked with this person, and, while he was talking, he was wiping the lather off of his face onto the towel. Then something happened that made him go back and turn the dog loose. That's when the person fired the shot. You can figure it all out, from the fact that there's lather on that towel, if you want to use your brain to think with, instead of thinking up a lot of foolish questions."

There was a moment of silence in the room, then a voice said, from the shadow which formed a circle beyond the beating illumination of the shaded incandescents: "Yes, I saw that towel."

"If," said Perry Mason, "you fellows would realize something of the significance of that towel, and preserve it as evidence, you might manage to figure out how that murder took place. You have that towel analyzed, and you'll find it's packed with shaving cream that had been wiped from Clinton Foley's face. You notice there's a little lather left on his chin, but not a great deal—not as much as would be expected if he'd been shot while his face was lathered. Also, there's no trace of lather on the floor where his face was resting. I tell you, he wiped the lather off on that towel."

"I don't see what's to have kept him from wiping his face *before* he started out to see who was in the other room," Sergeant Holcomb protested, interested in spite of himself.

"Simply," said Perry Mason, "that he dropped the towel when he was unchaining the dog. If he had been going to unchain the dog in the first place, he wouldn't have wiped the lather from his face. He would have unchained the dog first, and then gone out and wiped the lather from his face."

"Well, then," said Sergeant Holcomb, "where's Arthur Cartright?"

"I don't know. I tried to find him earlier in the day. His housekeeper says he's gone away."

"Thelma Benton says that he ran away with Mrs. Foley," Sergeant Holcomb remarked.

"Yes," said Perry Mason, "she told me that."

"And that's what Clinton Foley told Pete Dorcas."

"So I understand," Mason said wearily. "Are we going to go over all that again?"

"No, we're not going over that again," snapped Sergeant Holcomb. "I'm simply telling you that it's exceedingly possible your client, Arthur Cartright, ran away with Mrs. Foley; that he heard from Mrs. Foley's lips a story of abuse she had suffered at the hands of her husband; that he went back, determined to kill Clinton Foley."

"And about the only evidence you've got to go on is the fact that Cartright was having some trouble with Clinton Foley and ran away with his wife. Is that right?"

"That's enough evidence to go on."

"All right," Perry Mason said, "I'm just going to puncture your theory right now. If that had happened, and Arthur Cartright went back, he would have gone back with the deliberate intention of killing Clinton Foley, isn't that right?"

"I suppose so, yes."

"All right. If he had done that, he would have gone into the house, seen Clinton Foley, pointed a gun at him and gone *bang, bang*, right away. He wouldn't have stood around and argued while Foley was wiping the lather from his face. He wouldn't have stood still and let Foley go back and unchain a savage police dog. The only trouble with you guys is that you find a dead man and immediately start looking for some one who would make a good suspect. You don't look at the evidence and try to see where that evidence points."

"Where does it point?" asked Sergeant Holcomb.

"Hell!" said Perry Mason wearily. "I've done damn near all the detective work on this case so far. I'm not going to do *all* of your work for you. *You're* the one that's drawing pay for the job; I'm not."

"From all we can understand," said Sergeant Holcomb, "you've drawn pretty good pay to date for everything that you've done in the case."

Perry Mason gave an audible yawn.

"That," he said, "is one of the relative advantages of my profession, Sergeant. It also has corresponding disadvantages."

"Such as?" Sergeant Holcomb asked curiously.

"Such as the fact that one gets paid entirely on one's ability," Mason remarked. "The only reason I collect good money for what I do, is because I've demonstrated my ability to do it. If the taxpayers didn't give you your salary check every month until you'd delivered results, you might have to go hungry a few months,—unless you showed more intelligence than you're showing on this case."

"That'll do," said Sergeant Holcomb in a voice that quivered with indignation. "You can't sit here and insult me like that. You're not going to get anywhere with it, Mason, and you might as well realize it. This isn't a case where you're just an attorney. Dammit! You're a suspect."

"So I gathered," Mason said. "That's the reason I made the remark."

"Look here," Holcomb announced, "either you are lying about going out there at eight-thirty, or else you're being deliberately vague about it so that you can confuse the issue. Now, an examination shows that Foley was killed around seven-thirty to eight o'clock. He'd been dead more than forty minutes when the Homicide Squad got there. All you've got to do is to show where you were between seven-thirty and eight, and you'll be out of it as a suspect. Why the devil don't you cooperate with us?"

"I'm telling you," said Perry Mason, "that I don't know just what I was doing at that time. I didn't even bother to look at my watch. I went out and had dinner, strolled around and smoked a cigarette, went to the office, and then went back down to the street, walked around a little bit, thinking and smoking, picked up a cruising cab and went out to keep my appointment."

"And the appointment was at eight-thirty?"

"The appointment was at eight-thirty."

"But you can't prove it."

"Of course not. Why the devil should I have to prove the time of every appointment I've made? I'm a lawyer. I see people by appointments. I make lots of appointments during the day. As a matter of fact, in place of being a suspicious circumstance, the fact that I can't prove the time of the appointment, is the one thing that shows the appointment was made in ordinary business routine.

"If I could produce a dozen witnesses to show you that I'd made an appointment to talk over something with Clinton Foley, you would immediately commence to wonder why I had gone to all that trouble to show the time of the appointment. That is, you would if you had any brains.

"Now, I'll tell you something else. What the hell was to have prevented me going out to the house at seven-thirty, killing Foley, taking a taxicab back uptown, picking up another taxicab, and coming out to the house at eight-thirty to keep my appointment?"

There was a moment of silence in the room, and then Sergeant Holcomb said, "Nothing, as far as I can see."

"That's just the point," said Perry Mason. "Only, in the

event I'd done that, I'd have been pretty much inclined to take the number of the taxicab that took me out there at eight-thirty, and to have had witnesses to the fact that my appointment was at eight-thirty, wouldn't I?"

"I don't know *what* you'd do," said Sergeant Holcomb irritably. "When you start in on a case you don't do anything logically. You just act goofy all the way through it. Why the devil don't you come through and be frank with us, and go home and go to bed and let us get working on the case?"

"I'm not stopping you from working on the case," Perry Mason said, "and I'm not particularly keen about having these lights blazing into my eyes while you detectives sit around and stare at my face, thinking you can find something in my facial expression that's going to give you a clew. If you'd turn out the lights and sit in the dark and think for a while, it would do you a damn sight more good than sitting around in a circle and looking at my face."

"Well, it's not a face I'm crazy about looking at," Sergeant Holcomb said irritably.

"How about Thelma Benton?" asked Perry Mason. "What was she doing?"

"She's got a complete alibi. She can account for every minute of her time."

"By the way," said Perry Mason, "what were you doing at that time, Sergeant?"

Sergeant Holcomb's voice showed surprise.

"Me?" he asked.

"Sure, you."

"Are you going to try and make me a suspect?" he asked.

"No," said Perry Mason. "I was just asking you what you were doing."

"I was on my way up to the office, here," said Sergeant Holcomb. "I was in an automobile, somewhere between the house and the office."

"How many witnesses can you bring to prove it?" asked Mason.

"Don't be funny," Sergeant Holcomb told him.

"If you'd use your noodle, you'd see that I'm not being funny," Mason remarked. "I'm serious as hell. How many witnesses can you bring to prove it?"

"None, of course. I can show when I was at my house, and I can show the time I arrived at the office."

"That's the point," said Mason.

"What is?" asked Sergeant Holcomb.

"The point that should make you suspicious about this perfect alibi of Thelma Benton's. Whenever a person can show an iron-clad alibi covering what they've been doing every minute of the time, it's usually a sign that they've taken a great deal of care to perfect an alibi. A person who does that either participates in the commission of a murder and fakes an alibi, or else knows a murder is going to be committed, and therefore takes great pains to make a perfect alibi."

There was a long moment of silence. Then Sergeant Holcomb said, in a voice that was almost meditative, "So you think Thelma Benton knew Clinton Foley was going to be murdered?"

"I don't know anything at all about what Thelma Benton knew or didn't know," Perry Mason remarked. "I merely told you that a person who has a perfect alibi usually has a reason for it. In the ordinary run of a day's business, a person doesn't have an alibi for every minute of the time. He can't prove where he was, any more than you can prove it. I'll bet there isn't a man in the room who can prove, absolutely, by witnesses, what he was doing every minute between seven-thirty and eight o'clock tonight."

"Well," Holcomb remarked wearily, "it's a cinch *you* can't."

"Sure," said Mason, "and if you weren't so dumb, that

would be the best proof of my innocence, instead of an indication of my guilt."

"And you can't prove that you went to the house at eight-thirty. There's no one who saw you go there; no one knows you had an appointment? No one who let you in? No one who saw you there at all at eight-thirty?"

"Sure," said Perry Mason, "I can prove that."

"How?" asked Sergeant Holcomb.

"By the fact," Perry Mason said, "that I called police headquarters shortly after eight-thirty and told them about the murder. That shows I was there at eight-thirty."

"You know that isn't what I mean," Sergeant Holcomb told him. "I mean can you prove that you just came there at eight thirty?"

"Certainly not, we've already gone over that."

"I'll say we've gone over it," Sergeant Holcomb said. He scraped back his chair and got to his feet.

"You win, Mason," he said. "I'm going to let you go. You're pretty well established here in town, and we can put our finger on you whenever we want you. I don't mind telling you that I don't really think you did the murder, but I sure as hell think you're shielding some one, and that some one is a client of yours. I'm just going to tell you that in place of shielding your client, your conduct has made me all the more suspicious."

"Suppose you tell me just how," Mason said.

"I believe," said Sergeant Holcomb slowly, "that Arthur Cartright ran away with Foley's wife; that she told him a story of abuse, and that Cartright came back and shot Foley. Then I think that Cartright called you and told you what he'd done, and wanted to surrender himself; that you told him not to make a move until after you got there; that you went out and started Cartright going some place in a hurry, while you waited fifteen or twenty minutes, and then telephoned the police. In fact, there's no reason why *you* couldn't have been the one to have wiped off the dead man's face, and put the towel with the lather on it under the bathtub, near the dog chain."

"What's that make me? An accessory after the fact, or something of the sort?" asked Perry Mason.

"You're damn right it would," said Sergeant Holcomb, "and if I can ever prove it, I'm going to give you the works."

"I'm glad to hear you say so," said Perry Mason.

"Glad to hear me say what?" rasped Sergeant Holcomb.

"That you're going to give me the works *if* you can prove it. The way you've been acting, I thought you intended to give me the works whether you could prove anything or not."

Sergeant Holcomb gestured wearily. "Go ahead," he said, "and get out of here. Hold yourself in readiness so we can get you for further questioning, if we want to."

"All right," Perry Mason said, "if that's the way you feel about it, and if the interview's over, switch out this damned light. I've got a headache from it now."

CHAPTER X

PERRY MASON sat in Paul Drake's office. Paul Drake teetered in a creaky swivel chair, behind a small, battered desk. Against the far wall of the office two men sat, uncomfortably, in stiff-backed chairs.

"What," asked Paul Drake, "was the idea?"

"The idea in what?" Mason wanted to know.

"The idea in having me call the men off."

"I simply had everything that I wanted, and I didn't want the men to be found in the neighborhood."

"What was happening in the neighborhood?" Drake inquired.

"I don't know," Perry Mason said. "I didn't even know anything was going to happen, but I thought it might be a good idea to have the shadows called in."

"Listen," said Drake querulously, "there's a lot about this thing you're not telling me."

"Is that so?" asked Perry Mason, lighting a cigarette. "I thought you were supposed to find out things to tell me; not that I was supposed to find out things to tell you. Are these the two men who were on the job?"

"Yes. The man on the left is Ed Wheeler, and the other one is George Doake."

Perry Mason looked over at them.

"What time did you boys go on?" he asked.

"Six o'clock."

"Both of you were there all the time?"

"Most of the time. One of us would go and telephone every fifteen minutes."

"Where were you fellows? I didn't see you when I came up."

"We saw you all right," said Wheeler with a grin.

"Where were you?" Mason repeated.

"We were quite a distance from the house," Wheeler admitted, "but we were where we could see everything that went on. We had night glasses, and we were out of sight. There's a vacant house half way down the block, and we were in a room in the vacant house."

"Don't ask how they got in," said Paul Drake in his slow drawl. "That's a professional secret."

"All right," Mason said, "we'll each of us keep our professional secrets. What I want you boys to do is to tell me exactly what happened."

Ed Wheeler took out a leather-backed notebook from his coat pocket, thumbed the pages and said, "We went on duty at six o'clock. At about six-fifteen, the housekeeper, Thelma Benton, went out."

"Did she go out the front door or the back door?" asked Mason.

"Out the front door."

"All right, where did she go?"

"There was a man called for her in a Chevrolet car."

"Get the license?" Mason asked.

"Sure. It was 6M9245."

"What kind of a car—coupé, sedan or roadster?"

"A coupé."

"Go ahead. What next?"

"Then things were quiet. Nobody came and nobody left, until seven twenty-five. It was really a little past that—almost seven twenty-six, but I called it seven twenty-five. A Checker taxicab came to the place, and a woman got out."

"Did you get the number of the cab?"

"I didn't get the license number. The cab number was painted on the side of the car, and was easier to get than the license number, so I got that."

"What was it?"

"86-C."

"There's no chance that you're mistaken on that?"

"None. We both of us had night glasses and we both of us checked it."

"That's right," rumbled the other detective. "We're positive about the license numbers and all that stuff."

"All right, go on," said Mason.

"A woman got out and went into the house, and the cab went away."

"And it didn't wait?"

"No, it didn't wait. But it came back after twelve minutes. Evidently, the woman had sent the driver some place, and told him to do something and then come back."

"Go ahead," Mason said. "How about the woman? What did she look like?"

"We can't tell exactly. She was well dressed, and had on a dark fur coat."

"Did she wear gloves?"

"She wore gloves."

"Did you see her face?"

"Not plainly. You see, it was dark by that time. The street light showed the taxicab pretty plainly, and that made a shadow right where the woman got out. Then she walked rapidly up the walk, to the house, and went in."

"Did she ring the bell?"

"Yes, she rang the bell."

"Was she a long time about getting in?"

"No, she went in in just a minute or two."

"Looked as though Foley had been expecting her?"

"I don't know. She went to the house and paused for a minute at the front door, and then went in."

"Wait a minute," said Mason. "You say she rang the doorbell. How do you know?"

"I saw her bending over by the door. I figured that was what she was doing."

"Couldn't she have been opening the lock with a key?"

"Yes, she *could* have done that," said Wheeler. "Come to think of it, maybe that's what she was doing. I figured at the time she was ringing the bell, because that's what I expected her to do."

"Is there any chance the woman could have been Thelma Benton?"

"I don't think so. When Thelma Benton left she was wearing a different kind of coat. This woman wore a long black fur coat."

"How long was she in there?" asked the lawyer.

"She was in there fifteen minutes—maybe sixteen minutes. I've got the cab marked as driving away right after she went in. Then the cab came back in twelve minutes, and the woman left at seven forty-two."

"Did you hear any commotion? Dogs barking, or anything?"

"No, we didn't. But we wouldn't have heard anything anyway. You see, we were a ways down the block. It was the best place we could find to watch. The chief told us that he wanted us to be absolutely certain we weren't spotted. We probably could have come up a little closer after it got dark, but during the daytime we'd have been spotted in a minute if we hung around the place. So we got in this house that was down the street, and used binoculars to see what was going on."

"Go ahead," said Perry Mason. "What happened next?"

"After the woman drove away, nothing happened, until you showed up. You came in a yellow cab, and the cab number was 362. You got in there at eight twenty-nine, according to my watch, and we don't know what happened after that. We telephoned in to Drake, and Drake told us to get off the job right away and come in to the place here, but as we were driving away, we heard a bunch of sirens, so we wondered if anything had happened."

"All right," Mason told him, "don't wonder. It's not what you're paid to do. You're paid to watch, do you understand?"

"Yes."

"Well, then," Mason said, "here's what I want. I want you to round up that Checker driver, number 86-C, and bring him up to the place here. No, wait a minute, don't bring him up to the place. Get him spotted and telephone me here. I'll go talk with him myself."

"Anything else?"

"Not right away," said Perry Mason. He turned to Paul Drake.

"You're moving heaven and earth to get a line on these people I told you about?"

Drake nodded. "I think I've got something for you, Perry," he said, "but let's get rid of these boys first."

"On your way," Mason told them. "Get down to the Checker office. Find out who's running 86-C, and get him spotted for me, then telephone the office here just as soon as you've got him spotted. Another thing, it might be a good plan for you boys not to listen to any gossip while you're on the job."

"How do you mean?" Drake asked.

"I mean," Mason said, "that I don't want these boys

getting mixed into anything, other than being a couple of private dicks, working for day wages. Do you get me?"

"I think I get you," said Drake. "You boys understand?"

"We understand," Wheeler said.

"Get started then," said Mason.

He watched the two men as they left the office, his face set and stern, as though carved from granite, his steady eyes containing a smoldering light in their somber depths.

When the door had closed he turned to Paul Drake.

"Paul," he said, "there was a telegram sent from Midwick to Clinton Foley. That telegram purported to have been signed by the woman who had posed as Foley's wife, and asked him not to do anything criminally against Cartright. I want to get a photostatic copy of that telegram. Do you suppose you can work it?"

"It's going to be a job," Drake said.

"Never mind how much of a job it is; I want you to get it."

"I'll do what I can, Perry."

"Get started on that now."

Paul Drake reached for a telephone, paused a moment, then said, "I'd better go in another office and put that call through. Stick around, I've got something to tell you."

"I've got lots to tell you," Perry Mason said, "only I'm not going to tell you right now."

Drake stepped through a communicating door to another office, closed the door behind him, was gone five minutes, returned and nodded to Mason.

"I think I can fix it," he said.

"All right," Mason said. "Now tell me what you've found out. . . ."

The telephone rang. Paul Drake made a gesture for silence, scooped up the receiver, said "Hello," then listened.

"Got the address?" he asked at length.

He nodded his head, then turned to Mason.

"Make a note of this, will you, Perry? There's paper over there on the desk, and a pencil."

Mason walked to the desk, picked up a piece of paper, and held a pencil over it.

"Shoot," he said.

Paul Drake said in a slow voice, "Breedmont Hotel— B-r-e-e-d-m-o-n-t Hotel. Ninth and Masonic. Room 764, and the name is Mrs. C. M. Dangerfield, is that right?" He paused for a moment, then nodded to Perry Mason.

"That's it, Perry," he said. "That's all."

He slipped the receiver back on its hook.

"Who's that?" asked Perry Mason.

"That," said Paul Drake, "is the name under which Mrs. Bessie Forbes is registered at a hotel here in the city. Do you want to go see her? The room number is 764."

Perry Mason heaved a sigh of relief, folded the paper and thrust it in his pocket.

"Now," he said, "we're commencing to get some place."

"You want to go see her now?" asked Paul Drake.

"We've got to see that taxi driver first," Mason told him. "We'll have to get him up here now. There's no time for me to go to him."

"Why is the taxi driver so important?"

"I want to see that taxi driver, and see him first," Mason said. "Also, I want to get a shorthand reporter to take down the conversation. I have an idea I've got to get Della Street back to the office."

Paul Drake grinned at him.

"You don't need to worry about that girl," he said, "she's back at the office. She telephoned in a little while ago to see if I'd heard anything from you, and I told her you'd sent in an S O S to pull the shadows off the Foley house, and that I thought it was something important, so she said she was coming down to the office and stick around awhile."

Perry Mason nodded his head slowly.

"That," he said, "is the kind of cooperation that counts."

The telephone rang again. Drake picked up the receiver, said "Hello," listened for a moment, then nodded to Perry Mason.

"The boys have located that cab driver, Perry," he said. "They haven't talked with him yet, but they've found out from the main office where he is. He just checked in with a report."

"Tell the boys to go and hire the cab; to take it to my office and bring the driver up with them. Make some excuse to bring him up. Tell him they've got a trunk or a suitcase to bring down—anything to get him up there. And tell 'em to do it right away."

Drake nodded, transmitted Mason's instructions over the telephone, hung up and looked at Mason.

"What's next?" he asked. "Do we go up to your office and wait?"

Perry Mason nodded.

CHAPTER XI

THE cab driver fidgeted uncomfortably in his chair, glanced at Perry Mason, then let his eyes slither away to the faces of the two detectives, then looked at Della Street.

Della Street, perched on the edge of a chair, knees crossed, notebook held open on the desk, smiled reassuringly at him.

"What's the idea?" the driver asked.

"Just want to find out some information from you," said Mason. "We're collecting some evidence in connection with a case."

"What sort of a case?" asked the driver.

Mason nodded to Della Street, and she touched her pen to the notebook, streaming off a series of cabalistic signs from the point of the pen.

"The case," said Perry Mason slowly, "was a case involving a neighborhood fight over a howling dog. It seems to have developed into complications. We don't know yet just how serious those complications are. I want you to understand that the questions I am about to ask you deal only with the neighborhood fight over the howling dog, and the resulting charges which were made back and forth."

The cab driver settled back in the chair.

"Suits me," he said. "My meter's running downstairs."

"That's all right," Mason told him. "You get paid for the meter, and you get five dollars on top of it. How does that satisfy you?"

"It will when I get the five dollars," the driver said.

Mason opened a drawer in the desk, took out a five dollar bill and passed it across to the driver.

The cabbie pocketed the money and grinned.

"Now then," he said, "go ahead and shoot."

"Around seven-fifteen, or perhaps a little earlier, you picked up a passenger who had you take her to 4889 Milpas Drive," said Perry Mason.

"So that's it, eh?" said the cab driver.

"That's it," Mason said.

"What do you want to know about it?"

"What did the woman look like?"

"Gee, chief, that's hard to tell. I remember she had on a black fur, and she had some peculiar kind of perfume. She left a handkerchief in the car, and I smelled it. I was going to turn the handkerchief in to the Lost and Found Department, if she didn't say something about claiming it."

"How tall was she?" asked Perry Mason.

The driver shrugged his shoulders.

"Can't you give us any idea?"

The driver looked around him with a bewildered air.

Perry Mason nodded to Della Street. "Stand up, Della," he said.

The girl stood up.

"Tall as this girl?" Mason asked.

"Just about the same build," the driver said, looking Della Street over with appreciative eyes. "She wasn't as pretty as this girl, and she may have been a little heavier."

"You remember the color of her eyes?"

"No, I don't. I thought they were black, but maybe they were brown. She had a peculiar voice. I remember she talked funny. She talked in a high-pitched voice, and talked fast."

"You don't remember very much about her, then?" said Mason.

"Not too much, boss. She was the type of woman that you wouldn't—that is, that I wouldn't. You know how it is. There's lots of Janes gets in a cab and starts getting friendly right away. Well, she wasn't the kind that got friendly. Then there's lots of Janes that get in a cab and are on the make. They usually come through with some kind of a business proposition. This Jane wasn't on the make."

"Notice her hands? Did she have any rings on?"

"She had black gloves," said the cab driver positively. "I remember because she had some trouble fumbling around in her purse."

"All right, you took her there, and then what did you do?"

"I took her there, and she told me to watch her until I saw her get into the house. Then I was to go some place to a public telephone and telephone a number and deliver a message."

"Go ahead," Mason said, "what was the number and what was the message?"

"It was a funny message."

"Did she write it out?"

"No, she just told me and made me repeat it twice, so that I'd get it straight."

"All right, go ahead; what was it?"

The driver took a notebook from his pocket and said:

"I wrote down the number. It was Parkcrest 62945, and I was to ask for Arthur, and tell him that he'd better go over to Clint's house right away, because Clint was having a showdown over Paula."

Perry Mason glanced over at Paul Drake. Paul Drake's eyes were suddenly thoughtful, and they stared at Perry Mason with concerned speculation.

"All right," the lawyer said. "Did you deliver the message?"

"No, I didn't. I couldn't get anybody to answer the telephone. I tried three times, and then I came back. I waited a minute or two, and the Jane came out and I took her back."

"Where did you pick her up?"

"I was cruising around at Tenth and Masonic Streets, and I picked her up there. She had me take her back to the same place I picked her up."

"What's your name?" asked Perry Mason.

"Marson—Sam Marson, sir, and I live at the Bellview Rooms. That's on West Nineteenth Street."

"You haven't turned in that handkerchief yet?" asked Perry Mason.

Marson fished in his side coat pocket, took out a dainty square of lace, held it up and sniffed appreciatively.

"That's the perfume," he said.

Perry Mason reached for the handkerchief, smelled of it, then handed it across to Paul Drake. The detective smelled of it and shrugged his shoulders.

"Let Della take a whiff, and see if she can tell us what the perfume is," Perry Mason said.

Drake passed the handkerchief over to Della. She smelled it, then handed it back to Drake, looked at Perry Mason and nodded.

"I can tell," she said.

"Well, what is it?" said Paul Drake.

Perry Mason shook his head almost imperceptibly.

Drake hesitated for a moment, then dropped the handkerchief into the side pocket of his coat.

"We'll take care of the handkerchief," he told the cab driver.

Perry Mason's voice was suddenly edged with impatience.

"Wait a minute, Drake," he said. "I'm running this show. Give the man back his handkerchief. You don't own it."

Drake looked at Perry Mason with puzzled incomprehension upon his face.

"Go on," the lawyer said, "give it back. He's got to keep it for a while and see if she calls for it."

"Shouldn't I turn it in to the Lost and Found Department?" asked the cab driver, reaching for the handkerchief and putting it in his pocket.

"No," said Perry Mason, "not right away. Keep it for a while. I have an idea the same woman will probably show up and demand the handkerchief. When she does, ask her for her name and address, see? Tell her that you've got to make a report to the company, because you said over the telephone you had the handkerchief to surrender, and you'd have to find out the woman's name and address, or something like that. See?"

"Okay, I see," said the cab driver. "Anything else?"

"I think that's all," Mason told him. "We can reach you if we need you."

"You taking down everything I say?" asked the driver, looking over at the notebook in front of Della Street.

"Taking down the questions and answers," Perry Mason assured him casually. "So that I can show my client I've been on the job. It makes a difference, you know."

"Sure," said the cab driver, "we've all got to live. How about the meter?"

"One of the boys will go down with you and pay off the meter," Perry Mason said. "Be sure you take good care of that handkerchief, and be sure you get the name and address of the woman who claims it."

"Sure," said the cab driver, "that's a cinch."

He left the room and, at a nod from Paul Drake, the two detectives went with him.

Perry Mason turned to Della Street.

"What perfume, Della?" he asked.

"It just happens," said Della Street, "that I can tell you the name of that perfume, and I can also tell you that the young woman who wore it isn't a working girl—not unless she worked in pictures. I've got a friend in the perfume department of one of the big stores, and she let me smell a sample, just the other day."

"All right," said Mason; "what is it?"

"It's *Vol de Nuit*," said Della Street.

Perry Mason got to his feet, started pacing the office, head thrust forward, thumbs hooked in the arm holes of his vest. Abruptly he whirled on Della Street.

"All right," he said, "get this friend of yours, and get a bottle of that perfume. Never mind what it costs. Bust into the store if you have to. Get that just as soon as you can, and then come back to the office and wait until you hear from me."

"You got something in mind, Perry?" asked Paul Drake.

Mason nodded wordlessly.

"I don't want to say anything," said Drake, choosing his words carefully, and speaking with that characteristic drawl which gave the impression of a man to whom all forms of excitement had become a matter of routine, "but it seems to me that you're skating on thin ice. I'd like to know more what the sirens were doing, screaming out toward that Foley residence, before you got mixed into this thing too deep."

Mason studied Drake steadily for several seconds, and then said, "Were you going to tell me how to practice law?"

"I might tell you," said Paul Drake, "how to keep out of jail. I don't know law, but I know thin ice when I see it."

"A lawyer," said Perry Mason slowly, "who wouldn't skate on thin ice for a client ain't worth a damn."

"Suppose you break through?" Drake asked.

"Listen," Mason told him, "I know what I'm doing." He walked to the desk, took his forefinger and drew it along the blotter.

"There's the line of the law," he said. "I'm going to come so damn close to that line that I'm going to rub elbows with it, but I'm not going to go across it. That's why I want witnesses to everything I do."

"What are you going to do?" asked Drake.

"Plenty," said Perry Mason. "Get your hat; we're going to go places."

"Such as?" Drake wanted to know.

"The Breedmont Hotel," said Perry Mason.

CHAPTER XII

THE seventh floor of the Breedmont Hotel was a wide vista of polished doors. The corridor was wide and spacious, well lit with a soft light that came from indirect lighting fixtures. The carpet in the corridor was deep and springy.

"What was the room number?" asked Perry Mason.

"764," Drake told him. "It's around the corner, here."

"Okay," the lawyer said.

"What do you want me to do?" Drake asked.

"Keep everything shut except your eyes and your ears, unless I give you a tip to cut in on the conversation," Mason said.

"I get you," Drake remarked. "Here's your door."

Perry Mason knocked on it.

For several seconds there was no sound from the interior of the room. Mason knocked again, and then there was the rustle of motion, the sound of a bolt clicking, and a high-pitched feminine voice, speaking with nervous rapidity, said, "Who is it?" The door opened a bare crack.

"An attorney who wants to see you on a matter of importance," Perry Mason said in a low voice.

"I don't want to see any one," said the high-pitched voice, and the door started to close.

Perry Mason's foot blocked the door, just before the latch clicked into position.

"Come on, Paul," he said, and put his shoulder to the door.

A woman gave a high, hysterical scream, struggled for a moment, and then the door abruptly yielded.

The two men walked into the hotel bedroom as a partially clad woman staggered off balance, stared at them in white-faced panic, and abruptly snatched a silk kimono from the back of a chair.

"How dare you!" she blazed.

"Close the door, Paul," said Perry Mason.

The woman gathered the robe around her, walked determinedly to the telephone.

"I," she said, "am about to telephone to the police."

"Never mind about that," Perry Mason told her. "The police will be here soon enough."

"What are you talking about?"

"You know what I'm talking about," Perry Mason said. "You're about at the end of your rope—Mrs. Bessie Forbes."

At the name, the woman stood stiff and erect, staring at them with eyes that were dark with panic.

"Good God!" she said.

"Exactly," said Perry Mason. "Sit down now, and talk sense. We've got just a few minutes to talk, and I've got to tell you a lot. You've got to listen and cut out all this monkey business."

She dropped into a chair, and her excitement was such that the dressing gown fell open and remained unnoticed, disclosing the gleam of a bare shoulder, the luster of a sheer silk stocking.

Perry Mason stood with his feet planted apart, his shoulders squared, and snapped words at the woman, as though they had been missiles.

"I know all about you," he said. "There's no need to make any denial or go for any heroics or hysterics. You were the wife of Clinton Forbes. He left you in Santa Barbara and ran away with Paula Cartright. You tried to follow them. I don't know what your object was. I'm not asking you that, yet. Cartright located Clinton Forbes before you did. Forbes was living on Milpas Drive, under the name of Clinton Foley. Cartright got the house adjoining him, but didn't make his identity known. He was pretty well broken up. He was watching all the time, trying to find out whether Forbes was making his wife happy.

"I don't know just when you found out about it, or just how you found out about it, but it wasn't very long ago that you got wise to the whole situation.

"Now then, here's the funny thing. I'm a lawyer. You may have read of me. I've tried a few murder cases, and I expect to try some more. I specialize on criminal trial work on the big cases. My name's Perry Mason."

"You!" she said, in a tone of breathless interest. "You? You're Perry Mason?"

He nodded.

"Oh!" she breathed. "Oh, I'm *so* glad."

"Forget all that," he said, "and remember we've got an audience. I'm going to tell you a lot of stuff while I've got a witness here. You're going to listen and do nothing else. Do you get me?"

"Yes," she said, "I guess I understand what you want, all right, but I'm so glad to see you. I wanted . . ."

"Shut up," he told her, "and listen."

She nodded.

"Cartright," said Perry Mason, "came to my office. He acted strangely. He wanted to make a will. We won't talk about the terms of that will—not yet. But with the will came a letter and a retainer. The letter instructed me to protect the interests of the wife of the man who was living at 4889 Milpas Drive, under the name of Clinton Foley. Now get that, and get it straight. He didn't tell me to protect the woman who was going under the name of Mrs. Foley at 4889 Milpas Drive, but he told me to protect the lawfully wedded wife of the man who was going under the name of Clinton Foley, at that place."

"But did he understand just what he was doing? He wouldn't—"

"Shut up," Mason said. "Time's precious. I've got a witness to listen to what I say to you. I know what that's going to be. But I may not want a witness to what you say to me, because I don't know what you're going to say. Understand? I'm a lawyer, trying to protect you.

"Now Arthur Cartright mailed me a substantial retainer, with instructions to protect you and see that your legal rights were safeguarded. I've got the fee, and I propose to earn it. If you don't want my services, all you've got to do is to say so, and I walk out right now."

"No, no," she said, in a shrill, high-pitched voice. "I want your services. I need them. I want . . ."

"All right," Perry Mason said. "Now, then, can you do what I tell you to?"

"If it isn't too complicated," she said.

"It's going to be hard," he said, "but it isn't going to be complicated."

"Very well," she said. "What is it?"

"If anybody," he told her, "questions you about where you were at any time tonight, or what you were doing, tell them that you can't answer *any* questions unless your attorney is present, and that I'm your lawyer. Now, can you remember that?"

"Yes. That won't be hard to do, will it?"

"It may be," he told her, "and if they ask you how I became your lawyer, or when you hired me, or anything of that sort, simply make the same answer. And make the same answer to *all* questions. If they ask you what the weather is. If they ask you how old you are. If they ask you what kind of face cream you use, or anything else, make the same answer. Do you understand that?"

She nodded.

Perry Mason abruptly walked to the fireplace.

"What's been burning here?" he asked.

"Nothing," she said.

Perry Mason leaned over the fireplace and stirred the ashes in the grate.

"Smells like some kind of cloth," he said.

The woman said nothing, but stared at him in white-faced silence.

Perry Mason picked up a small piece of cloth. It was silk, green, and printed with a brown triangle.

"Looks like part of a scarf," he said.

She took a swift step toward him.

"I didn't know . . ."

"Shut up!" he said, whirling on her.

He took the singed bit of cloth, put it in his vest pocket, then pulled the grate out of the fireplace, and started poking through the ashes. After a moment, he straightened, walked to the dressing table, picked up a bottle of perfume, smelled it, walked swiftly to the wash stand, pulled the cork, and dumped the perfume down the wash stand.

The woman gasped, moved toward him, and put a restraining hand on his arm.

"Stop!" she said. "That stuff costs . . ."

He whirled on her with eyes that were blazing.

"It's likely to cost a hell of a lot," he said. "Now listen to this and get it straight: Check out of this hotel. Go to the Broadway Hotel on Forty-Second Street. Register under the name of Bessie Forbes. Be careful what you take with you, and be careful what you leave behind. Buy yourself some good cheap perfume, and when I say cheap, I mean cheap. Souse it all over everything you've got. Do you get me?"

She nodded.

"Then what?" she asked.

"Then," he said, "sit tight and don't answer any questions. No matter who asks you a question or what it's about, say you won't do anything until your lawyer is present."

He turned on the hot water tap, washed out the perfume bottle, kept the hot water running.

The room gave forth a fragrance of perfume, and Perry Mason turned to Paul Drake.

"Better smoke, Paul," he said. "A cigar if you've got one."

Paul Drake nodded, pulled a cigar from his pocket, clipped off the end and struck a match to it. Perry Mason walked across to the windows, raised the windows, and nodded to the woman.

"Get some clothes on," he said. "My telephone number is Broadway 39251. Make a note of it. Call me if anything happens. Remember that my services aren't going to cost you a cent. They're all paid for. Remember that you're going to answer all questions asked of you, no matter what they may be, with just that one answer, that you can't talk unless your lawyer tells you to.

"Have you got that straight?"

She nodded.

"Have you got guts enough," he asked, "to stand on your two feet, look the world squarely in the eyes, and tell them you won't answer a single question unless your lawyer is there?"

She lowered her eyes and looked thoughtful.

"Suppose," she said, "that they tell me that would work against me? That is, isn't it supposed to be an admission of guilt for a person to make a statement like that? Not that I'm guilty of anything, but you seem to think that . . ."

"Please," he said, "don't argue with me. Have enough confidence in me to do as I tell you. *Will* you do that?"

She nodded.

"All right," he told her. "That's all, Drake. Come on." He turned, pulled open the door of the room, paused on the threshold to give her a parting instruction.

"When you check out of here," he said, "don't leave a back trail. Go to the depot and buy a ticket some place. Then switch redcap porters, pick up another taxicab and go to the place I told you and register under the name I told you. You got that straight?"

She nodded.

"All right," said Mason. "Come on, Paul."

The door banged behind them.

In the corridor Paul Drake looked at Perry Mason.

"You," he said, "may think that you're keeping on one side of the line, but it looks to me as though you've gone over."

"Think I've broken through the thin ice, Paul?" asked Perry Mason.

"Hell," said Paul Drake explosively, "you're in ice water up to your chin right now, and it's getting deeper."

"Stick around," Perry Mason told him, "you haven't seen anything yet. Here's what I want you to do. I want you to get me an actress, about twenty-eight years old, about the same build as that woman, and have her at my office just as quick as you can get her there. She's going to make three hundred dollars for doing something, and I'm going to guarantee that it's going to be within the law. I don't want you to be there personally, and don't want you to know anything about it. I simply want you to get the actress and send her to me. I want you to get a girl who will do anything. You understand? Anything."

"How much time have I?" asked Paul Drake.

"You've got less than ten minutes, if you can do it in that time. I know you can't, but you've got to do it just as fast as you can. You've got a list of people that you can call on to do various jobs, and what you've got to do is to check over it, get the right person, and get in touch with her."

"I've got a girl," said Paul Drake slowly, "who might answer the description. She worked as a lure on the vice squad for a while, and knows her way around. She'd do anything."

"Is she light or dark?"

Paul Drake smiled slowly.

"She," he said, "is about the same build and complexion as Mrs. Bessie Forbes. That's the reason I thought of her."

"All right," Mason said, "don't get too damn smart, or it might not be so good. This is a case where you're going to be dumb. The dumber the better. Remember, I'm the one that's giving orders. You're just following them, and you don't know anything yet."

"I'm commencing to suspect a lot," Paul Drake said.

"Suspect all you want to, but don't tell me anything about it, and keep your thoughts to yourself, because you're going to want to forget them later on."

"Okay," said Drake, "You go on up to your office, and I'll get this girl to show up. Her name's Mae Sibley. You don't need to mince words with her."

"Okay," said Mason, "get started—and thanks, Paul."

CHAPTER XIII

MAE SIBLEY was well-built and attractive. Perry Mason stood close to her, looked her over with approval.

"Give me that bottle of perfume, Della," he said.

He took the bottle of perfume, wafted it beneath the young woman's nostrils.

"Any objection to using this?" he asked.

"I'll say not, I could use all of that you wanted to give me."

"All right, put on lots of it."

"Where?"

"On your clothes—anywhere."

"I hate to waste that good perfume."

"That's all right, go ahead and put it on."

Della Street smiled at the young woman, and said, "Perhaps I can help."

She applied perfume liberally to the girl's clothes.

"Now," said Perry Mason, "you're going to go to a certain taxicab and tell the driver that you left a handkerchief in the taxicab. When you had him take you out to 4889 Milpas Drive. Do you suppose you can remember that?"

"Sure. What else do I do—anything?"

"That's all, just take the handkerchief and give the cab driver a sweet smile."

"Then what?"

"He'll give you the handkerchief and ask you for your address. Because, he'll tell you, you've got to let him know where you live so he can report to the Lost and Found Department."

"Very well, then what do I do?"

"Then you give him a phoney name and address, and fade from the picture."

"That's all there is to it?"

"That's all there is to it."

"What name and address do I give him?"

"Give him the name of Agnes Brownlie, and tell him that you live at the Breedmont Hotel, on Ninth and Masonic Streets. Don't give him any room number."

"What do I do with the handkerchief?"

"After you've got the handkerchief, you bring it to me."

"This is on the up and up?" she asked.

"It's within the law," he told her, "if that's what you want to know."

"And I get three hundred dollars for doing it?"

"Three hundred dollars when the job is finished."

"When's the job going to be finished?"

"There may not be anything more to it," he told her,

"but you've got to keep in touch with me so that I can reach you at any time. Give me your telephone number and arrange so that I can reach you on short notice any time I want to."

"And how do I find the taxicab driver?"

"In exactly fifteen minutes," Perry Mason told her, "the taxicab driver will come up to the corner of Ninth and Masonic Streets, and telephone in to his office to find out if there are any calls for him. The particular taxi that you want is a Checker cab, number 86-C. You telephone in to the head office of the taxicab company, tell them that you left an article in the cab, and ask them to let you know where the cabbie is as soon as he reports. Leave them a number so they can call you back. They'll call you back in fifteen minutes, when he reports, and tell you that he's at Ninth and Masonic. You tell them that you're right near there, so you'll go and pick him up. Pretend that you recognize him. You can spot him from the number on the cab. Be a little friendly with him."

"Okay," she said, "anything else?"

"Yes," he told her, "you've got to talk in a peculiar tone of voice."

"What sort of tone of voice?"

"High and fast."

"Like this?" she asked, raising her voice, and saying rapidly: "I beg your pardon, but I think I left my handkerchief in your taxicab."

"No," he said, "that's too high and not fast enough. Try it a little lower, and you've got to drag out the ends of the words a little bit more. You're clipping them off too much. Put kind of a little emphasis on the word ends."

Mae Sibley watched him closely, her head cocked slightly on one side, in the attitude of a bird listening. She closed her eyes.

"Like this?" she asked: "I beg your pardon, but didn't I leave my handkerchief in your taxicab?"

"That's a little more like it," he said, "but you've got

108

to do it more like this. Now listen: 'I beg your pardon, but didn't I leave my handkerchief in your taxicab?'"

"I think I get you," she said. "It's a trick of talking rapidly until you come to the last word in each phrase, and then you drawl out the end of it."

"Maybe that's it," he said. "Go ahead and try it. Let's see how it works."

She flashed him a sudden smile. "I beg your pardon," she said, "but I think I left my handkerchief in your taxicab."

"That's it," he told her. "It's not perfect, but it's good enough. Now get started. You haven't got much time. Della, you've got a black fur coat hanging in the closet. Give it to her. Okay, go ahead. Put on your coat, sister, and then grab a taxi and beat it out to the Breedmont Hotel. You can call the cab office from there. They'll have the cab reporting in about ten minutes now. You've just about got time to put through your calls and make it, and make it snappy."

He ushered her to the door, turned to Della Street, and said, "Get Paul Drake on the line, and tell him to come up here right away."

She nodded, and her fingers worked the dial of the telephone.

Perry Mason started pacing back and forth across the office, his face immobile, his stare fixed.

"He'll be right up," she said. "What is it, chief, can you tell me?"

Perry Mason shook his head.

"Not yet, I can't, Della. I'm not certain, myself, just what it is."

"But what's happened?"

"Plenty," he told her, "and the trouble is it doesn't fit together."

"What's bothering you?" she asked.

"I am wondering," he said, "why that dog howled, and why he quit howling. Sometimes I think I know why the dog howled, and then I can't figure why he quit howling. Sometimes I figure that it's *all* goofy."

"You can't expect things to dovetail together too accurately," she told him, her eyes dark with concern. "You've just come out of one big case, and now you're plunging right in on another."

"I know it," he told her. "It's something of a strain, but I can stand it all right. That isn't what's bothering me. What's bothering me is why the facts don't fit together. Don't ever fool yourself that facts don't fit, if you get the right explanation. They're just like jigsaw puzzles—when you get them right, they're all going to fit together."

"What doesn't fit in this case?" she asked.

"Nothing fits," he said, then glanced up as there was a knock at the outer door.

"Paul Drake, I guess," he said.

He strode to the door, opened it, and nodded to the tall detective.

"Come in, Paul," he said. "I want you to get the dope on the man that Thelma Benton went out with; the man who drove the Chevrolet coupé, 6M9245."

Paul Drake's smile was slow and good-natured.

"Don't think you're the only one that can put any pep into your work," he said. "I've had my men working on that, and already have the answer for you. The fellow is Carl Trask. He's a young man who's drifted around and had a police record. Right at present he's engaged in doing some small-time gambling."

"Can you find out anything more than that about him?"

"In time, yes. We're getting stuff. In fact, we're getting stuff coming in from all over the country. We've got a lot more reports on the situation in Santa Barbara. I've checked down everybody who was in the household—even including the Chinese cook."

"That's right," Perry Mason said. "I'm interested in that cook. What happened to him?"

"They made some kind of a deal with him, by which

he agreed to be deported. I don't know just what it was. I think that Clinton Foley got in touch with the Federal authorities to find out what it was all about; found there was no question but what the boy was in this country illegally. So Foley worked out a deal by which the Chink was to be deported at once, without being held for further examination or trial, and gave him enough money to set himself up in some sort of business in Canton. Our money buys a lot of Chinese money, at the present rate of exchange, and money means a lot more in China."

"Find out anything else about him?" asked Perry Mason. "That is, the cook?"

"I found out that there's something funny about the tip-off that caused the Federal authorities to go out there and round him up."

"What sort of a tip-off was it?"

"I don't know exactly, but, from all I can gather, some man telephoned and said that he understood Ah Wong was in the country without a proper certificate; that he didn't want to disclose his identity or have his name used in any way, but he wanted something done about it."

"Chinese or white man?" asked Perry Mason.

"Apparently a white man, and apparently rather well educated. He talked like an educated man."

"Well," said Mason, "go on."

"That's all there is, definite," said the detective, "but one of the clerks in the immigration office handled that anonymous tip, and also talked with Foley over the telephone. She's got a goofy idea that it was Foley who gave the tip-off."

"Why would Foley do that?" Mason asked.

"Search me," said the detective, "probably there's nothing to it. I'm simply telling you what the clerk told me."

Perry Mason took a package of cigarettes from his pocket, gave one to Della Street, then to Paul Drake. He lit Della's cigarette, then Drake's, and would have lit his own from the same match, but Della Street stopped him.

He smoked in silence for several minutes.

"Well," said Drake at length, "what are we here for?"

Perry Mason said, "I want you to get handwriting specimens from Paula Cartright; from Cartright's housekeeper; and from this woman, Thelma Benton. I'm going to get a sample from Bessie Forbes."

"What's the idea?" asked the detective.

"I'm not ready to talk yet," Mason said. "I want you to wait here for a while, Paul." And he began pacing the floor, restlessly.

The others watched him in silence, respecting the concentration of his thoughts. They finished their cigarettes, pinched out the stubs. Mason still continued his restless pacing.

The telephone rang after some ten or fifteen minutes, and Della Street answered it, then looked up to Perry Mason, holding the receiver in her hand.

"It's Miss Sibley," she said, "and she wants me to tell you that she did exactly as you instructed, and that everything is all right."

"Has she got the handkerchief?" asked Perry Mason.

Della Street nodded. Perry Mason showed excitement.

"Tell her to get a cab and come over to the office right away," he said; "to bring that handkerchief with her, and pay the cab driver to make time. But be sure and tell her not to get that Checker cab. Get another cab."

"What's it all about?" asked Paul Drake.

Perry Mason chuckled.

"You stick around about ten minutes," he said, "and you'll find out. I'm about ready to let the lid off."

Paul Drake settled back in the big leather chair, slid his long legs over the arm of the chair, put a cigarette in his mouth, and scraped a match on the sole of his shoe.

"Well," he said, "I can stick it out if you can. I guess you lawyers never sleep."

"It's not so bad after you get used to it," Mason said,

and resumed his pacing of the floor. Once or twice he chuckled, but, for the most part, he paced in silence.

It was following one of those chuckles, that Paul Drake drawled a question.

"Going to let me in on the joke, Perry?"

"I was simply thinking," Perry Mason said, "how delightfully surprised Detective Sergeant Holcomb is going to be."

"Over what?" asked Drake.

"Over the information I'm going to give him," Mason replied, and resumed his steady pacing of the floor.

The knob on the outer door rattled, and there was a gentle knock on the panels.

"See who it is, Della," said the lawyer.

Della Street went swiftly to the door, opened it, and let Mae Sibley into the room.

"Have any trouble?" asked Perry Mason.

"Not a bit," she said. "I just told him what you told me to say, and he took me for granted. He looked me over rather closely, and asked me a few questions. Then he took the handkerchief from his pocket and gave it to me. He was slick enough to smell the handkerchief and then smell my perfume, to make sure they matched."

"Good girl," Mason said, "and you gave him the name of Agnes Brownlie?"

"Yes. And the address, Breedmont Hotel—just like you told me."

"All right," Perry Mason said, "you get one hundred and fifty dollars now, and one hundred and fifty dollars a little later. You understand that you're not to say a word about this."

"Of course."

Perry Mason counted out the money.

"You want a receipt?" she asked.

"No," he told her.

"When do I get the other hundred and fifty?"

"When the job's finished."

113

"What else have I got to do?"

"Perhaps nothing. Perhaps you'll have to go to court and testify."

"Go to court and testify?" she said. "Over what?"

"Over exactly what happened."

"Not tell any lies?"

"Certainly not."

"How soon will you know?" she asked.

"Probably in a couple of weeks. You've got to keep in touch with me. That's all. You'd better get out of here now, because I don't want you to be seen around the office."

She extended her hand. "Thanks a lot for the work, Mr. Mason," she said. "It's appreciated."

"You don't know how much I appreciate what you've done," he told her.

It was evident that there was a vast change in the lawyer's manner, a relief that was disclosed in his bearing. He turned to Della Street, as the door of the outer office closed on Mae Sibley.

"Get police headquarters," he said, "and get Detective Sergeant Holcomb on the line."

"It's pretty late," she reminded him.

"That's all right. He works nights."

Della Street got the connection through, then looked up at her employer.

"Here's Detective Sergeant Holcomb on the line," she said.

Perry Mason strode to the telephone. He was smiling as he picked up the receiver.

"Listen, Sergeant," he said; "I've got some information for you. I can't give it all to you, but I can give you some of it. . . . Yes, some of it is professional confidence, and I can't give you that. I think I understand the duties of an attorney and the rights and liabilities of an attorney. An attorney is supposed to guard the confidences of his client, but he's not supposed to compound a crime. He's not supposed to suppress any evidence. He can keep anything that his client tells him to himself, provided it's something that was necessary to a preparation of the case he's handling or related to the advice he's giving a client...."

Mason ceased talking for a minute and frowned while the receiver made squawking noises. Then he said in a conciliatory tone: "That's all right, Sergeant. Keep your shirt on. I'm not making any dissertation on the law; I'm simply telling you so that you'll understand that which I'm going to tell you now. It happens that I've just found out that a Checker cab, number 86-C, took a woman to Clinton Foley's house at about twenty-five minutes past seven. The woman was there for about fifteen or twenty minutes. The woman left a handkerchief in the taxicab. Now that handkerchief undoubtedly is evidence. That handkerchief is now in my possession. I'm not at liberty to explain to you how it came in my possession, but it's here, and I'm going to send it over to police headquarters . . . all right, you can send over for it if you want. I won't be here, but my secretary, Della Street, will be here, and she'll give it to you . . . yes, the taxicab driver can undoubtedly identify it. . . . I can tell you this much: the woman who rode in the taxicab dropped a handkerchief, or left it in the cab. The driver found it. Later on, the handkerchief came into my possession. I can't tell you how I got it. . . . No, damn it, I can't tell you that. . . . No, I won't tell you that. . . . I don't give a damn what you think. I know my rights. That handkerchief is evidence, and you're entitled to it, but any of the knowledge that I have received from a client is a sacred communication, and you can't drag it out of me with all the subpœnas on earth."

He slammed the receiver back on the hook, tossed the handkerchief over to Della Street.

"When the officers come," he said, "give them this, and
115

don't give them anything else except a sweet smile. Keep any information you have to yourself."

"What happened?" she asked.

Perry Mason stared at her steadily.

"If you insist on knowing," he said, "Clinton Foley was murdered between seven-thirty and eight o'clock tonight."

Paul Drake pursed his lips into a silent whistle.

"In one way," he said, "you haven't surprised me, and in another you have. When I first heard about those sirens, I figured that's what might have happened. Then, when I saw the stuff you were doing, I figured even you wouldn't take those kind of chances on a murder rap."

Della Street's eyes turned not to Perry Mason, but to Paul Drake.

"Is it that bad, Paul?" she asked.

The detective started to say something, then caught his breath and was silent.

Della Street walked to Perry Mason's side and looked up at him.

"Chief," she said, "is there anything I can do?"

His eyes softened as he looked down at her.

"This is something I've got to work out alone," he said.

"Are you going to tell the police," she asked, "about the man who wanted to know what effect it would have on his will if he was executed for murder?"

Perry Mason stared steadily at her.

"We," he said, "aren't going to tell the police anything other than what we've already told them."

Paul Drake snapped out words with unaccustomed vehemence:

"Perry," he said, "you've taken enough chances on this thing. If the person who murdered Clinton Foley consulted you beforehand, you've got to go to the police and . . ."

"The less *you* know about this situation," Mason said, "the fewer chances you'll be taking."

The detective's voice was lugubrious.

"I know too darn much already," he said.

Mason turned to Della Street.

"I don't think they'll question you," he said slowly, "if you tell them that I left you this handkerchief to give to them and that that's all you can tell them about it."

"Don't worry about me, Chief," she said. "I can take care of myself, but what are you going to do?"

"I'm going out," he said, "and I'm leaving right now."

He strode to the door, paused with his hand on the knob and looked back at the pair in the office.

"The things I've done," he said, "are all going to click together and make sense and they're also going to make one hell of a commotion. I've got to take chances. I don't want either of you to take any chances. I know just how far I can go; you don't. Therefore, I want you to follow instructions and stop."

Della Street's voice was quavering with worry.

"Are you sure you know where to stop, Chief?" she asked.

"Shucks," rasped Paul Drake, "he never knows where to stop."

Perry Mason jerked the door open.

"Where are you going from here, Perry?" asked the detective.

Mason's smile was serenely untroubled.

"That," he said, "is something it might be better for you not to know."

The door slammed shut behind him.

CHAPTER XIV

Perry Mason caught a cruising cab in front of the office.

"Get me to the Broadway Hotel on Forty-second Street," he said, "and make it snappy."

He settled back in the cushions and closed his eyes while the cab threaded its way through the streets that were now almost deserted. When the cab pulled up in front of the Broadway Hotel, Perry Mason tossed the driver a bill, strode across the lobby to the elevators, as though going upon important business. He got out at the mezzanine, called the room clerk, and said: "Will you give me the number of the room assigned to Mrs. Bessie Forbes?"

"Eight ninety-six," said the room clerk.

"Thanks," said Mason. He hung up the telephone, went to the elevator, got off at the eighth floor, walked to room 896 and rapped on the door.

"Who is it?" asked Bessie Forbes's frightened voice.

"Mason," Perry Mason said in a low tone. "Open the door."

A bolt clicked, and the door opened. Mrs. Forbes, now fully clothed in a street costume, stared at him with eyes that showed fright, but were rigidly steady.

Perry Mason walked in and closed the door behind him.

"All right," he said, "I'm your lawyer. Now tell me exactly what happened tonight."

"What do you mean?" she asked.

"I mean about the trip you made to see your husband."

She shuddered, looked about her, motioned Perry Mason to a seat on the davenport. She came and sat down beside him, and twisted her fingers around a handkerchief. She was redolent of cheap perfume.

"How did you know I went out there?" she asked.

"I guessed it," he said. "I figured that you were about due to put in an appearance. I couldn't figure any woman who answered your description, who would make the kind of a call on Clinton Foley that you made, and then the description the taxi driver gave fitted you right down to the ground."

"Yes," she said slowly, "I went out there."

"I know you went out there," he said impatiently. "Tell me what happened."

"When I got there," she said slowly, "the door was

118

locked. I had a passkey. I opened the door and walked in. I wanted to see Clint without giving him time to prepare for my visit."

"All right," he said. "What happened? You went in there and then what happened?"

"I went in," she said, "and found him dead."

"And the dog?" asked Perry Mason.

"Dead."

"I don't suppose that you've got any way of showing that you didn't do the killing?"

"They were both dead when I got there," she said.

"Had they been dead long?"

"I don't know; I didn't touch them."

"What did you do?"

"I felt so weak I sat down in a chair. At first, all I could think about was running away. Then I remembered that I would have to be careful. I knew that I might be suspected of having done the shooting."

"Was the gun lying on the floor?" asked Perry Mason.

"Yes," she said, "the gun was lying on the floor."

"It wasn't your gun?"

"No."

"Did you ever have a gun like that?"

"No."

"Never saw that gun before?"

"No, I tell you I didn't have a thing to do with it. My God! won't you believe me? I couldn't lie to you. I'm telling you the truth."

"All right," he said; "we'll let it go at that. You're telling me the truth then. So what did you do?"

"I remembered," she said, "that the taxi driver had gone to telephone Arthur Cartright. I thought that Arthur would come over, and I knew that Arthur would know what to do."

"Did it ever occur to you that Arthur Cartright might have been the one who did the shooting?"

"Of course it did, but I knew that he wouldn't come over if he had been the one to do the shooting."

"He might have come over and blamed it on you."

"No, Arthur isn't that kind."

"Okay, then," Perry Mason said. "You sat down and waited for Cartright, and then what happened?"

"After a while," she said, "I heard the taxicab come back. I don't know how long it was. I had lost all track of time. I was all broken up."

"All right," he told her, "go on from there."

"I went out, got into the taxicab and drove back to the vicinity of my hotel. Then I got out. I figured that no one would ever be able to trace me. I don't know how you found out about it."

"Did you know," said Perry Mason, "that you left a handkerchief in the taxicab?"

She stared at him with eyes that kept getting wider and more terrified.

"Good God, no!" she said.

"You did," he told her.

"Where is the handkerchief?"

"The police have it."

"How did they get it?"

"I gave it to them."

"You *what*?"

"I gave it to them," he said. "It came into my possession, and I didn't have any alternative but to surrender it to the police."

"I thought you were acting as my lawyer."

"I am."

"That doesn't sound like it. Good God, that's the worst evidence that they could get hold of! They'll be able to trace me through that handkerchief."

"That's all right," Perry Mason told her. "They're going to trace you anyway, and they're going to question you. When they question you, you can't afford to lie to them. And you can't afford to tell them the truth. You're in a jam, and you've got to keep quiet. Do you understand that?"

"But that's going to prejudice everybody against me—the police, the public, and everybody."

"All right," he told her, "that's what I'm coming to. Now, I had to surrender that handkerchief to the police because it was evidence. The police are on my trail in this thing and they'd like to catch me doing something that would make me an accessory after the fact. They're not going to have that pleasure. But you've got to use your wits in order to get yourself out of this mess.

"Now here's what you do: The police are going to come here. They're going to ask you all sorts of questions. You tell them that you won't answer any questions unless your lawyer is present. Tell them that your lawyer has advised you not to talk. Don't answer any questions whatever. You understand that?"

"Yes, that's what you told me before."

"Think you can do it?"

"I guess so."

"You've got to do it," he said. "There are a lot of loose angles about this thing I can't check up on. I don't want you to tell anything until I know the entire story, and know how the facts fit in."

"But it's going to prejudice the public. The newspapers will say that I refuse to talk."

Perry Mason grinned.

"Now," he said, "you're commencing to get down to brass tacks. That's what I came to see you about. Don't tell the police anything. Don't tell the newspapers anything. But do tell them both that *you* want to talk, but that *I* won't let you. Tell them that I have told you you can't say a word. Tell them that *you* want to. Tell them that *you* want to explain. Tell them that you'd like to call me up and talk with me; that you think you can get my permission to talk, and all that sort of stuff. They'll give you a telephone and let you talk with me. You plead with me over the telephone for permission to talk. Tell me that you'd like to explain at least what you're doing here in the city; what happened in Santa Barbara; what your plans were. Beg with me, plead with me. Get tears in your voice. Do anything you want to. But I'll sit tight and tell you that the minute you tell anybody anything, you've got to get another lawyer. Do you understand that?"

"Do you think that will work?" she asked.

"Sure it'll work," he said. "The newspapers have got to have something for a story. They'll try to get something else. If they can't get anything else, they'll pick on that and spread it all over the front page that you want to tell your story, and I won't let you."

"How about the police? Will they release me?"

"I don't know."

"Good heavens! You don't mean I'm going to be arrested? My God! I can't stand that! I could probably stand being questioned if they questioned me here in my room. But if they took me down to the jail, down to police headquarters, and questioned me, I'd go crazy. I simply can't stand anything like that, and I can't afford to be put on trial. You don't suppose there's any chance I'm going to be put on trial, do you?"

"Now, look here," he told her, getting to his feet and standing facing her, his eyes steady and insistent. "Don't pull that stuff with me. It doesn't get you anywhere. You're in a jam, and you know it. You went into your husband's house. You let yourself in with a passkey. You found him dead on the floor. You realized that he'd been murdered. There was a gun there. You didn't notify the police. You went to a hotel and registered under an assumed name. If you think you can pull a stunt like that, and not get taken down to police headquarters, you're crazy."

She started to cry.

"Tears aren't going to do you any good," he said, with brutal frankness.

"There's only one thing that'll do you any good, and that's using your noodle and following the instructions I give you. Don't ever admit that you were at the Breedmont Hotel, or that you were ever registered anywhere under an assumed name. Don't admit anything except that you have retained me, and that you won't answer any questions or make any statements unless I am present and advise you to do so. The only exception you make to that is to complain bitterly to the newspapers that *you* want to tell your story, and that *I* won't let you. Do you get all that?"

She nodded.

"All right," Mason said. "That disposes of the preliminaries. Now, there's one other thing . . ."

Knuckles sounded imperatively on the door of the room.

"Who knows you're here?" asked Perry Mason.

"No one," she said, "except you."

Perry Mason motioned her to keep silent. He stood staring at the door in frowning concentration.

The knocks were repeated, this time louder and with a peremptory impatience.

"I think," said Perry Mason, in a low tone of voice, "that you've got to get yourself together. Remember, what they do with you is entirely up to you. If you can keep your head, I can do you some good."

He walked to the door, twisted the bolt and opened it. Detective Sergeant Holcomb, flanked by two men, stared at Perry Mason in amazed surprise.

"You!" said the officer. "What are you doing here?"

"I," said Perry Mason, "am talking with my client, Bessie Forbes, widow of Clinton Forbes who lived at 4889 Milpas Drive under the name of Clinton Foley. Does that answer your question?"

Sergeant Holcomb pushed into the room.

"You're damn right it does," he said, "and I know

now where you got that handkerchief. Mrs. Forbes, you're under arrest for the murder of Clinton Forbes, and I want to warn you that anything you say may be used against you."

Perry Mason stared with grim-faced hostility at the officer.

"That's all right," he said, "she won't say anything."

CHAPTER XV

PERRY MASON entered his office, freshly shaved, eyes clear, step springy, to find Della Street engrossed with the morning newspapers.

"Well, Della," he said, "what's the news?"

She stared at him with a puzzled frown on her face.

"Are you going to let them do that?"

"Do what?"

"Arrest Mrs. Forbes?"

"I can't help it. They've already arrested her."

"You know what I mean. Are you going to let them charge her with murder and keep her in jail while her trial's coming up?"

"I can't help it."

"Yes, you can, too, you know you can."

"How?"

"You know as well as I do," she said, getting to her feet and pushing the paper across the surface of her desk, "that Arthur Cartright is the man who killed Clinton Foley, or Clinton Forbes, if you want to call him by his real name."

"Well," said Perry Mason, smiling, "how well do you know it?"

"I know it so well that there even isn't any use talking about it."

"Well, then," he said, "why talk about it?"

She shook her head. "Look here, Chief," she said; "I've got confidence in you. I know you always do the square thing. You can make all the wise cracks you want to, but you still can't convince me that it's right to let this woman stay in jail, just so Arthur Cartright can get a good head start on the police. It's bound to come out sooner or later. Why not give this woman a break and let it come out now? Cartright's had plenty of head start, and, after all, you're almost compounding a felony, being an accessory to the murder."

"In what way?" he asked.

"Withholding from the police the information you have about Mr. Cartright. You know perfectly well that he intended to murder Clinton Foley."

"That doesn't mean anything," Perry Mason said slowly. "He might have intended to murder him, but that doesn't mean he did murder him. You can't accuse a man of murder without some evidence."

"Evidence!" she exclaimed. "What more evidence do you want? The man came in here and almost told you in so many words that he intended to commit a murder. Then he sends you a letter which shows he has perfected his plans and is intending to take action. Then he disappears completely, and the man who has wronged him is found murdered."

"Haven't you got the cart before the horse?" Perry Mason asked. "Shouldn't you say that he murdered the man and then disappeared, if you wanted to make a good case of it? Doesn't it sound rather strange to say that he disappeared, and that the man he had a grudge against was murdered after his disappearance, instead of before?"

"That's all right for you to talk that way to a jury," she said, "but you're not fooling me any. The fact that the man made his will and sent you the money showed that he was intending to take the final step in his campaign. You know what that final step was, as well as I do. He had been watching and spying on the man who broke up his home, waiting for an opportunity to make his presence known to the woman in the case. That opportunity came.

He took the woman away from the house and put her in a safe place. Then he came back, did the job, and joined the woman."

"You forget," Perry Mason told her, "that everything I know came to me in the nature of a professional confidence. That is, all the statements Cartright made."

"That all may be," she said, "but you don't have to sit back and let an innocent woman be accused of crime."

"I'm not letting her be accused of crime," he retorted.

"Yes, you are," she said. "You've advised her not to talk. She wants to tell her story, but she doesn't dare to, because you've told her not to talk. You're representing her, and yet you're letting her be wronged, just so this other client of yours can make good his escape."

Perry Mason sighed, smiled, shook his head.

"Let's talk about the weather," he said. "It's more tangible."

She moved over toward him, and her eyes were indignant.

"Perry Mason," she said, "I worship you. You've got more brains and more ability than any other man I know. You've done things that have been simply marvelous, and now you're doing something that is just a plain, downright injustice. You're putting a woman on the spot, just so you can protect Cartright's interests. They're going to catch him sooner or later, and they're going to try him, and you figure that if you can make the police get off on the wrong scent in the meantime, you've strengthened Cartright's case."

"Would you believe me," he asked, "if I told you you were all wet?"

"No," she said. "Because I know I'm not."

He stood staring down at her, chin thrust forward aggressively, eyes smoldering.

"Della," he said, "the police could have built up a good case of circumstantial evidence against Cartright, *if* they knew as much as we know. But don't ever fool your-

126

self that they can't build up a good case of circumstantial evidence against Bessie Forbes."

"But," she said, "you talk only of cases. Arthur Cartright is guilty. Bessie Forbes is innocent."

He shook his head patiently, doggedly.

"Listen, Della," he said; "you're trying to take in too much territory. Remember that I'm a lawyer. I'm not a judge, and I'm not a jury. I only see that people are represented in court. It's the function of the lawyer for the defense to see that the facts in favor of the defendant are presented to the jury in the strongest possible light. That's all he's supposed to do. It's the function of the district attorney to see that the facts in favor of the prosecution are presented to the jury in the most favorable light. It's the function of the judge to see that the rights of the parties are properly safeguarded, that the evidence is introduced in a proper and orderly manner; and it's the function of the jury to determine who is entitled to a verdict. I'm a lawyer, that's all. It's up to me to present the interests of my clients to the best of my ability, so that the best possible case can be made out. That's my sworn duty. That's all I'm supposed to do.

"If you'll stop and analyze the whole system of justice that we have built up, you'll find that there's nothing else for a lawyer to do. Lots of times the lawyer for the defendant gets a little too clever, and people condemn him. They overlook the fact that the district attorney is as clever a lawyer as the state can find. And the lawyer for the defense has to counteract the vigor of the prosecution by putting up as shrewd and plausible a defense as he can. That's the theory under which our constitutional rights are given to the people."

"I know all that," she said, "and I understand how often the ordinary layman gets a false idea of what it's all about. He doesn't understand just what an attorney is supposed to do, or just why it's so necessary that he does it. But that still doesn't answer the question in this case."

Perry Mason extended his right hand, clenched it, opened it, and then clenched it again.

"Della," he said, "I hold in that hand the weapon which will strike the chains from the wrists of Bessie Forbes, and send her out into the world a free woman, but I have got to use that weapon in a certain way. I have got to strike at just the right time, and in just the right manner. Otherwise, I will simply dull the edge of my weapon and leave the woman worse off than she is now."

Della Street looked at him with eyes that contained a glint of admiration.

"I love to hear you talk that way," she said. "It thrills me when that tone comes into your voice."

"All right," he said, "keep it under your hat. I hadn't intended to tell you—now you know."

"And you promise me you're going to use that weapon?" she asked.

"Of course I'm going to use it," he said. "I'm representing Bessie Forbes, and I'm going to see that she gets the best I can give her."

"But," she said, "why not strike now? Isn't it easier to beat a case before it's been built up?"

"He shook his head patiently.

"Not this case, Della," he said. "It's a stronger case against her than any one realizes. That is, a shrewd man can make a strong case of it. I don't dare to strike until I know the full strength of that case. I can only strike once. I've got to do it so dramatically that it will make the one blow sufficient. I've got to get the public interested in Bessie Forbes first. I've got to build up sympathy for her.

"Do you know what it means to build up sympathy for a woman who is charged with murder? If you get off on the wrong foot, the newspapers send special reporters out to interview her as a tiger woman, as a lioness. They write columns of drivel about the feline grace with which she moves, the leonine glint that comes in her eyes, the hidden ferociousness which lurks under a soft exterior.

"Right now I'm making a bid for public interest. I'm making a bid for public sympathy. I want the public to read the newspapers and realize that here is a woman of refinement who has been thrown in jail, charged with murder; who can establish her innocence, and who wants to do it, but who is prevented by the orders of an attorney."

"That will make sympathy for the woman, all right," Della Street pointed out, "but it's going to put you in a bad light. The public will think you're simply grandstanding for the purpose of getting a big fee out of the trial."

"That's what I want the public to think," he told her.

"It's going to hurt your reputation."

He laughed mirthlessly.

"Della," he said, "just a moment ago you were picking on me because I wasn't doing enough for the woman. Now you've switched around and are jumping on me because I'm doing too much."

"No," she said, "that isn't right. You can do it in another way. You don't need to sacrifice your reputation in order to protect her."

He moved toward the inner office.

"I wish to God I didn't," he said, "but there's no other way. Get Paul Drake on the 'phone and tell him to come in here; I want to see him."

Della Street nodded, but made no move toward the switchboard until after Perry Mason had closed the door of his inside office. Then she picked up the telephone.

Perry Mason flung his hat on the top of a bookcase and started pacing the floor. He was still pacing the floor when Della Street opened the door and said: "Here's Paul Drake."

"Send him in," Mason told her.

Paul Drake regarded Perry Mason with eyes that held his usual lazy twinkle.

"Gosh, guy," he drawled, "don't you *ever* sleep?"

"Why?" asked Perry Mason.

"I crossed your back trail last night. Or rather, my men did," Drake told him.

"I got a couple of hours sleep," Mason said, "and a good Turkish bath and a shave. That's all I need when I'm working on a case."

"Well," said Drake, dropping into a big leather chair and sliding his knees around so that his legs hung over the arm, "give me a cigarette and tell me what's new."

Mason handed him a package of cigarettes, held a match for him.

"You want lots of service," he said.

"So do you," Drake remarked. "You've got every private detective agency in the country boiling in a turmoil. I've had more telegrams of misinformation and immaterial facts than you could digest in a week."

"Have you found any trace of Arthur Cartright or Paula Cartright?" asked Mason.

"Not a trace. They've vanished from the face of the earth. What's more, we've covered every taxicab agency in the city, talked with every taxicab driver, and we can't find any one who made the trip out to 4889 Milpas Drive that morning, when Mrs. Cartright left Foley's place."

"You don't know what kind of a taxicab it was?"

"No. Thelma Benton says it was a taxicab. She's certain of that, but we can't find the taxicab."

"Perhaps the driver is lying," Mason said.

"Perhaps, but it isn't likely."

Mason sat down behind his desk and made drumming motions with his fingers on the surface of the desk.

"Paul," he said, "I can beat that case against Bessie Forbes."

"Of course you can," Drake told him. "All you've got to do is to let the woman tell her story. What's the idea of keeping her silent? That's a dodge that's used only by guilty people or hardened criminals."

"I want to make certain that your men can't find Cartright before I have her tell her story," Perry Mason said.

"What's that got to do with it?" asked Drake. "Do you think Cartright is guilty and you want to make certain he's where the police can't find him before you let police attention get diverted from Bessie Forbes?"

Perry Mason made no answer to the question, but sat silent. After a moment he started pounding gently with his right fist on the desk.

"Paul," he said, "I can bust that case wide open. But in order to do it I've got to strike at the psychological moment. I've got to build up public interest, and I've got to get a dramatic tension built up, and then I've got to strike so fast that the district attorney can't think up the answer before the jury brings in a verdict."

"You mean that woman is going to trial?"

"I mean," said Perry Mason, "she's *got* to go to trial."

"But the district attorney doesn't want to try her. He's not certain he's got a case. He wants her to tell her story. That's all he wants."

Perry Mason spoke slowly and emphatically. "That woman," he said, " has got to be tried, and, of course, she's got to be acquitted. But it won't be easy."

"I thought you said you could bust the case wide open."

"I can, if I can strike at the right time and in the right manner, but I've got to be spectacular about it."

"Why not try to get her off on her preliminary examination?"

"No, I'm going to consent that she be bound over for trial, and I'm going to ask for an immediate trial."

Paul Drake blew out cigarette smoke and regarded the lawyer quizzically.

"What's this weapon you've got that you're holding back?" he asked.

"You probably wouldn't think much of it if I told you," said Mason.

"Well you might try me."

"I'm going to," Mason said, "because I've got to. That weapon is a howling dog."

Paul Drake whipped the cigarette from his lips with a gesture of swift surprise, and stared at Perry Mason with eyes that had lost their twinkle of lazy humor.

"For heaven sake," he said, "are you still harking back to that howling dog?"

"Yes," Mason said.

"Shucks, that's out of the case long ago. The dog's dead, and it didn't howl."

Perry Mason said, doggedly, "I want to establish the fact that the dog *did* howl."

"But what difference does it make?"

"A lot of difference."

"It's just a silly superstition anyway," Paul Drake said. "Nothing that would have bothered anybody in particular, except a person who was mentally weak, like this man Cartright."

"I have *got* to establish," said Perry Mason doggedly and determinedly, "that the dog *did* howl. I have got to prove it by evidence. The only evidence that I dare to rely on is that of Ah Wong, the Chinese cook."

"But Wong says the dog didn't howl."

"Wong has got to tell the truth," said Perry Mason. "Have they deported him yet?"

"They're leaving with him today."

"All right," said Perry Mason. "I'm going to get out a subpœna naming him as a witness and hold him here. Then I want you to get some clever Chinese interpreter. I want you to impress upon that interpreter the necessity of getting Ah Wong to admit that the dog did howl."

"You mean you want him to *say* the dog howled whether the dog howled or not?"

"I mean," said Perry Mason, "that I want Ah Wong to tell the truth. That dog howled. I want to establish it. But don't get me wrong. If the dog didn't howl, I want

Ah Wong to say so. But I'm satisfied the dog did howl, and I want to prove that he did."

"Okay," said Drake, "I think I can attend to that. I know some of the fellows in the immigration office."

"One other point," said Perry Mason. "I think it would be a good thing to spring it on Ah Wong that Clinton Foley, or Forbes, whichever you want to call him, was responsible for the arrest of Ah Wong. I think it might be a good idea to get that thing impressed pretty strongly on the oriental mind."

"I get you," said Paul Drake. "I haven't the faintest idea of what you're getting at, but I don't suppose that makes any difference. What else do you want?"

"I want," said Perry Mason slowly, "to find out everything I can about that dog."

"What do you mean?"

"I want to find out how long Clinton Forbes had owned that dog. I want to find out about the dog's habits. I want you to chase back over the dog's entire life and find out if he was ever known to howl at night.

"Now, when Clinton Foley first took that house at 4889 Milpas Drive, he had the police dog. Find out how long he'd had it, where he got it, how old the dog was. Find out everything about it, and, particularly, about the howling."

"I've already got some of that information," the detective said. "Forbes had had the dog for years. When Forbes left Santa Barbara he took the dog with him. That was one of the things he couldn't bear to leave behind. He was attached to the dog—so was his wife, for that matter."

"All right," said Perry Mason. "I want evidence to show all about that dog. I want witnesses who can come here and testify about him. I want witnesses who have known that dog from a pup. Go to Santa Barbara. Get the neighbors who would have heard the dog if he'd ever howled at night. Get affidavits from them. Some of them we'll want as witnesses. Spare no expense."

"All over a dog?" asked Paul Drake.

"All over a dog," Perry Mason said, "who didn't howl in Santa Barbara, but who did howl here."

"The dog's dead," the detective reminded him.

"That doesn't affect the importance of the evidence," Mason said.

The telephone rang. Mason picked up the receiver.

"One of Mr. Drake's detectives on the line, and he wants to report to him at once," Della Street said. "He says its important."

Perry Mason turned the receiver over to Paul Drake.

"One of the men with some more information, Paul."

Drake slid over to the edge of the chair arm, lifted the receiver to his ear and drawled a lazy "Hello."

The receiver made swift metallic noises, and a look of surprised incredulity came over Drake's face.

"You're sure about that?" he asked at length.

The receiver made more noises.

Drake said, "I'll be damned," and hung up the telephone. He looked at Perry Mason with eyes that still showed startled surprise.

"Know who that was?" he asked.

"One of your men?" asked Mason.

"Yes," said Drake, "one of my men who's covering the police headquarters, picking up tips from newspaper reporters, and all that stuff. Do you know what he told me?"

"Naturally," said Perry Mason, "I do not. Go ahead and spill it."

"He told me," said Paul Drake, "that the police have positively identified the gun that was found in Foley's house; the gun that killed the police dog and Foley."

"Go ahead," Mason said. "How did they identify it?"

"They identified it by tracing the numbers and getting the report on sales. They've found out definitely and positively who bought that gun."

"Spill it," Mason said; "go ahead and tell me. Who bought it?"

"The gun," said Paul Drake slowly, his eyes watching

Perry Mason's face in concentrated scrutiny, "was purchased in Santa Barbara, California, by Bessie Forbes, two days before her husband ran away with Paula Cartright."

Perry Mason's face became wooden. He stared at the detective in expressionless appraisal for nearly ten seconds.

"Well," said Drake, "what have you got to say?"

Perry Mason's eyes half closed.

"I'm not going to say anything," he said. "I'm going to take back something that I did say."

"What?"

"When I told you that at the proper moment I could bust that case against Bessie Forbes wide open."

"I," said Drake, "am doing a lot of mind changing, myself."

"It's all right," Mason said slowly. "I still *think* I can bust that case wide open, but I don't know."

He picked up the telephone, placed the receiver to his ear with a slow, deliberate motion, and when he heard Della Street's voice, said, "Della, get me Alex Bostwick, the city editor of *The Chronicle*. Get him on the line, personally. I'll wait."

The expression of surprise gradually faded from Paul Drake's eyes, and his face resumed once more its look of droll humor.

"Well," he said slowly, "that hands me a jolt. I'm commencing to think you either know more about this case than I thought you did, or else that you're crazy like a fox. Maybe it was a good thing Mrs. Forbes didn't rush out and make a lot of explanations to the police."

"Perhaps," Perry Mason said softly, then turned to the telephone. "Hello . . . this Bostwick? Hello, Alex, Perry Mason talking. I've got a hot tip for you. You always claimed that I never gave you tips so that your men could dig up a scoop. Here's one that's a pippin. Have a reporter go out to 4893 Milpas Drive. It's the residence of a man named Arthur Cartright. He'll find a housekeeper there

135

who is deaf and cranky. Her name's Elizabeth Walker. If your reporter will draw her out, he'll find that she knows who murdered Clinton Foley ... yes, Clinton Forbes, who lived at 4889 Milpas Drive, under the name of Clinton Foley. . . .

"Yes, she knows who did the killing. . . .

"No, it wasn't Bessie Forbes. You get her to talk. . . .

"All right, if you insist. She'll tell you that it was Arthur Cartright, the man for whom she works, and who has mysteriously disappeared. That's all. Goodby."

Perry Mason slid the receiver back on the hook and turned to Paul Drake.

"God! Paul," he said, "but I hated to do that."

CHAPTER XVI

THE room in the jail, set aside for conferences between attorneys and clients, contained no furniture other than a long table running the length of the room, flanked with chairs on either side. Midway along the table, stretching entirely through the table to the floor, and up to a height of five feet above the table, was a heavy wire screen.

An attorney and his client could sit on opposite sides of the table. They could see each other's faces, hear plainly what was said; but they could not touch each other; nor could they pass any object through the screen. The visiting room had three doors. One of them opened from the jailor's office to the side of the room where attorneys were admitted; one opened from the jailor's office to the side where prisoners were admitted, and one led from the prisoners' side of the room to the jail.

Perry Mason sat in a chair at the long table, and waited impatiently. His fingers made little drumming sounds upon the battered table top.

After a few moments the door from the jail opened and a matron walked into the room, with Mrs. Forbes on her arm.

Bessie Forbes was white-faced, but calm. Her eyes held a haunting expression of terror, but her lips were clamped together in a firm, determined line. She looked about the room, and then saw Perry Mason, as the attorney got to his feet.

"Good morning," he called.

"Good morning," she said, in a firm, steady voice, and walked over to the table.

"Take that seat across from me," said Perry Mason.

She sat down and tried a smile. The matron withdrew through the door which went to the jail. The guard peered curiously through the steel cage, then turned away. He was entirely out of ear-shot. Attorney and client were alone.

"Why," said Perry Mason, "did you lie to me about the gun?"

She looked about her with a haunted, hunted look, then moistened her lips with the extreme tip of her tongue.

"I didn't lie," she said. "I had just forgotten."

"Forgotten what?" he asked.

"Forgotten about purchasing that gun."

"Well, then," he said, "go ahead and tell me about it."

She spoke slowly, as though choosing her words carefully.

"Two days before my husband left Santa Barbara," she said, "I found out about his affair with Paula Cartright. I got a permit from the authorities to keep a gun in the house, went down to a sporting goods store, and bought the automatic."

"What did you intend to do with it?" he asked.

"I don't know," she said.

"Going to use it on your husband?"

"I don't know."

"Going to use it on Paula Cartright?"

"I don't know, I tell you. I just acted on an impulse. I think, perhaps, I was just going to run a bluff."

"All right," he said, "what happened to the gun?"

"My husband took it away from me."

"You showed it to him, then?"

"Yes."

"How did you happen to show it to him?"

"He made me angry."

"Oh, then you threatened him with it?"

"You might call it that. I took the gun from my purse and told him I'd kill myself before I'd be placed in the position of a neglected wife who hadn't been able to hold her husband."

"Did you mean it?" Perry Mason asked, studying her from expressionless, patient eyes.

"Yes," she said, "I meant it."

"But you didn't kill yourself."

"No."

"Why?"

"I didn't have the gun when it happened."

"Why didn't you?"

"My husband had taken it from me. I told you."

"Yes," said Mason, "you told me that, but I thought perhaps he'd given it back."

"No. He took it, and I never saw it again."

"So you didn't commit suicide because you didn't have the gun?"

"That's right."

Mason made drumming motions with his fingertips on the table top.

"There are other ways of committing suicide," he said.

"Not easy ways," she told him.

"There's lots of ocean around Santa Barbara."

"I don't like drowning."

"You like being shot?" he asked.

"Please don't be sarcastic. Can't you believe me?"

"Yes," he said slowly. "I'm looking at it from the standpoint of a juror."

"A juror wouldn't ask me those questions," she flared.

"No," Mason told her moodily, "but a district attorney would, and the jurors would be listening."

"Well," she said, "I can't help it. I've told you the truth."

"So your husband took that gun with him when he left?"

"I guess so. I never saw it again."

"Then your idea is that some one took that gun from your husband, killed the police dog and killed him?"

"No."

"What is your idea?"

"Some one," she said slowly, "who had access to my husband's things took that gun and waited the right opportunity to kill him."

"Who do you think that was?"

"It might," she said, "have been Paula Cartright, or it might have been Arthur Cartright."

"How about Thelma Benton?" said Perry Mason slowly. "She looks like rather an emotional type to me."

"Why should Thelma Benton kill him?" asked the woman.

"I don't know," said Perry Mason. "Why should Paula Cartright have killed him, after she lived with him so long?"

"She might have had reasons," said Bessie Forbes.

"According to that theory, she would have first run away with her husband, then returned and killed Forbes."

"Yes."

"I think," said Perry Mason slowly, "it would be better to stick to the theory that Arthur Cartright killed him, or that Thelma Benton killed him. The more I see of it, the more I'm inclined to concentrate on Thelma Benton."

"Why?" she asked.

"Because," he told her, "she's going to be a witness against you, and it's always a good move to show that a witness for the prosecution might be trying to pass the crime onto somebody else."

"You don't act as though you believed what I tell you," she said, "about the gun."

139

"I never believe anything that I can't make a jury believe," Perry Mason told her. "And I'm not certain that I can make a jury believe that story about the gun, if they also believe that you went there in a taxicab; that you saw your husband's dead body lying on the floor, and made no move to report to the police, but that you fled from the scene of the murder and tried to conceal your identity by taking a room under the name of Mrs. C. M. Dangerfield."

"I didn't want my husband to know I was in town."

"Why not?" he asked her.

"He was utterly cruel and utterly ruthless," she answered.

Perry Mason got to his feet and motioned to the attendant that the interview was over.

"Well," he said, "I'll think it over. In the meantime, write me a letter and tell me that you've been giving your case a great deal of thought, and that you want to tell your story to the newspaper reporters."

"But I've already told them that," she said.

"Never mind that," Perry Mason told her, as the matron appeared through the door leading from the jail. "I want you to put it in writing and send it to me."

"They'll censor it before it goes out of the jail?" she asked.

"Of course," he told her. "Good-by."

She stood staring at him until he had left the visitors' cage, her expression that of puzzled bewilderment.

The matron tapped her arm.

"Come," she said.

"Oh," sighed Bessie Forbes, "he doesn't believe me."

"What's that?" asked the matron..

"Nothing," said Mrs. Forbes, clamping her lip in a firm, straight line.

Perry Mason stepped into the telephone booth, dropped a coin and dialed the number of Paul Drake's detective bureau.

After a moment he heard Drake's voice on the line.

"Paul," he said, "Perry Mason talking. I'm going to shift my guns in that murder case a little."

"You don't need to shift them any; you've got them covering every point in the case now," Drake told him.

"You haven't seen anything yet," Mason remarked. "And I want you to concentrate on Thelma Benton. She's got an alibi that covers every minute of her time, from the time she left the house, until she got back. I want to find a hole in that alibi some place, if I can."

"I don't think there's any hole in it," Drake said. "I've checked it pretty thoroughly, and it seems to hold water. Now I've got some bad news for you."

"What is it?"

"The district attorney has found out about Ed Wheeler and George Doake, the two detectives who were watching Clinton Foley's house. They've got deputies out looking for them."

"They got wise to those birds through the taxi driver," Perry Mason said slowly.

"I guess so," said Drake.

"The deputies found them?"

"No."

"Are they likely to?"

"Not unless you want them to."

"I don't want them to," said Perry Mason. "Meet me at my office in ten minutes, and have all the reports on this Thelma Benton."

He heard Drake sigh over the telephone.

"You're getting this case all mixed up, brother," Drake told him.

Perry Mason laughed grimly.

"That's the way I want it," he said, and hung up the receiver.

Perry Mason caught a taxicab to his office, and found Paul Drake waiting for him with a sheaf of papers.

Mason nodded to Della Street, took Paul Drake's arm and piloted him into the inner office.

"All right, Paul," he said. "What have you found out?"

"There's only one weak point in the alibi," the detective said.

"What's that?"

"That's this fellow Carl Trask, the gambler who showed up in the Chevrolet and took Thelma Benton from the house. She was with him at various places until eight o'clock. I've checked the times when they showed at the various places. There's a gap between seven-thirty and seven-fifty. Then they drifted into a speak and had a drink. Trask left shortly after eight o'clock, and the girl went to a booth and had dinner by herself. The waiter remembers her perfectly. She left about eighty-thirty, picked up a girl friend and went to a picture show. Her alibi is going to depend on Carl Trask's testimony from around seven-thirty to seven-fifty, and on the girl friend from eight-thirty on.

"But we don't care about busting the alibi after eight-thirty. Between seven-thirty and seven-fifty is the time you want to concentrate on, and from all I can find out, that's going to rest on Carl Trask's testimony, and, of course, that of Thelma Benton herself."

"Where does she claim she was?" Mason asked.

"She says she was down at another speak, having a cocktail, but nobody remembers her down there. That is, nobody has yet."

"If," said Perry Mason moodily, "she could find somebody down there who remembered her, it would give her a pretty good alibi."

Paul Drake nodded wordlessly.

"And," said Perry Mason slowly, "if she can't, it's going to be a weak spot, if we can impeach Carl Trask in some way. You say he's a gambler?"

"Yes."

"Any criminal record?"

"We're looking it up. We know he's been in minor troubles."

"All right, look him up from the time he was a kid down to date. Get something on him if you can. If you can't, get something that won't sound good to a jury."

"I'm already working on that," Drake said.

"And the deputies are looking for Wheeler and Doake?"

"Yes."

"By the way," said Perry Mason casually, "where *are* those two birds?"

Paul Drake looked at Perry Mason, and his face held the innocence of a child.

"I had a very important matter to investigate in Florida," he said, "and I put those two fellows on a plane and sent them there on the job."

"Anybody know they went?" asked Perry Mason.

"No. It's a confidential matter, and they didn't get tickets in their own names."

Perry Mason nodded appreciatively.

"Good work, Paul," he said.

He made little drumming gestures with his fingertips on the desk, abruptly said, "Where can I reach Thelma Benton?"

"She's staying at the Riverview Apartments."

"Under her own name?"

"Yes."

"You keeping her shadowed?"

"Yes."

"What's she doing?"

"Talking with cops, mostly. She's made three trips to headquarters and two to the district attorney's offices."

"For questioning?"

"I don't know whether they're in response to telephone communications or not. But there was only once she was sent for. The rest of the time she went by herself."

"How's her hand?" asked Mason.

"I don't know that. It's pretty well bandaged. I chased down the doctor who treated it. His name's Phil Morton and his offices are in the Medical Building. He was called out to the house on Milpas Drive, and said the hand was pretty badly mangled."

"Mangled?" asked Perry Mason.

"Yes, that's what he said."

"She still has it bandaged?" asked the lawyer.

"Yes."

Abruptly, Perry Mason took down the telephone.

"Della," he said, "ring up the Riverview Apartments. Get Thelma Benton on the line. Tell her that this is *The Chronicle* speaking, and the city editor wants to talk with her. After that has soaked in, put her on my line."

He hung up the telephone.

Drake looked at him without expression on his face and said slowly, "You're skating on pretty thin ice, Perry."

Perry Mason nodded gloomily.

"I've got to," he said.

"How about that line?" asked Drake. "Are you still on the right side of it?"

The lawyer gave his shoulders a nervous shake, as though trying to rid himself of a disagreeable sensation.

"I hope so," he said.

The telephone rang.

Perry Mason picked up the receiver, raised his voice, and snapped: "City Editor."

The receiver made metallic noises, and then Perry Mason still speaking in the same high-pitched rapid tone of voice said: "Miss Benton, it looks as though this Forbes murder case is going to have a lot of dramatic interest. You've been with the parties from the start. Did you keep a diary?"

Once more the receiver made metallic noises, and a slow smile spread over the face of Perry Mason.

"Would you be interested in ten thousand dollars for the exclusive right to publish that diary . . . you would? . . . Have you kept your diary up to date? . . . will you keep it right up to date? . . . Don't say anything about this offer.

I'll have one of our reporters get in touch with you when we want it. I can't tell about the price until I take it up with the managing editor. Then he'll want to inspect the diary, but I'm willing to make a recommendation for its purchase at that figure, provided we have the exclusive on it. That's all. G'by."

Mason slammed the receiver up on the line.

"Think she'll try to trace that call?" asked the detective.

"She can't," Mason said. "What's more, she hasn't got sense enough. She fell for it, hook, line and sinker."

"She keeps a diary?" asked the detective.

"I don't know," Perry Mason said.

"Didn't she say she did?"

Perry Mason laughed.

"Sure," he said, "she said she did but that doesn't mean anything. The way I made the offer, she is going to have time to fake one. A girl can do a lot of writing for ten thousand dollars."

"What's the idea?" asked Drake.

"Just a hunch," Mason said. "Now let's check over those samples of handwriting. Have you got samples of handwriting?"

"I haven't got a sample of Mrs. Forbes' handwriting, but I have got a sample of Paula Cartright's handwriting. I've got some stuff that Thelma Benton has written, and a letter that Elizabeth Walker, Cartright's housekeeper, wrote."

"Have you checked them," Perry Mason said slowly, "with the note that was left by Paula Cartright when she left Forbes?"

"No, the district attorney's office has got that note, but I have a photostatic copy of the telegram that was sent from Midwick, and the handwriting doesn't check."

"What handwriting doesn't check?"

"None of them."

"That telegram's in a woman's handwriting?"

Drake nodded, fished through the folder, and took out a photostatic copy of a telegram.

Mason took the paper and studied it carefully.

"Does the telegraph operator remember anything about it?" he asked.

"He just remembers that a woman handed it in, across the counter, together with the exact amount necessary to send it. She seemed in very much of a hurry. The telegraph operator remembers that he was counting the words when she started out. He told her he'd have to check the amount, and she called over her shoulder that she was quite sure it was right, and went out."

"Would he remember her again if he saw her?"

"I doubt it. He's not too intelligent, and apparently didn't pay any particular attention to her. She came in wearing a wide-brimmed hat. The operator remembers that much. She had her head tilted down so that the brim kept him from seeing her face when she was handing the telegram across the counter. After that, he started to count the words, and she walked out."

Mason continued to stare at the photostatic copy of the telegram, then glanced up at Drake.

"Drake," he said, "how did the newspapers get onto the inside of all this business?"

"What inside?"

"All about the man who lived under the name of Foley being, in reality, Clinton Forbes, and having run away with Paula Cartright, and the Santa Barbara scandal end of the thing?"

"Shucks," said Drake, "that was a cinch. We found it out, and it's a cinch the newspapers were as well organized as we were. They have correspondents in Santa Barbara, and they dug up the files of old newspapers and made a great human interest story out of it. Then, you know the district attorney—he likes to try his cases in the newspapers. He's been feeding them everything he could find out."

Perry Mason nodded his head thoughtfully.

"Drake," he said, "I think I'm getting about ready to go to trial."

The detective looked at him with some show of surprise.

"The case won't be tried for some time yet, even if you try to get an immediate hearing," he said.

Perry Mason smiled patiently.

"That," he said, "is the way to prepare a criminal case. You've got to make all of your preparations and block out your defense before the district attorney really finds out what it's all about. After that, it's too late."

CHAPTER XVII

THE courtroom atmosphere was stale with that psychic stench which comes from packed humans whose emotions are roused to a high pitch of excitement.

Judge Markham, veteran judge of the criminal department, who had presided over so many famous murder trials, sat behind the massive mahogany rostrum with an air of complete detachment. Only a skilled observer would have noticed the wary watchfulness with which he filtered the proceedings through his mind.

Claude Drumm, chief trial deputy of the district attorney's office, tall, well-tailored, suave, was very much at his ease. Perry Mason had inflicted stinging defeat before but in this case the prosecution was certain of a verdict.

Perry Mason sat at the counsel table, with an air of indolent listlessness about him which marked a complete indifference to the entire case. His attitude was in contrast to the accepted attitude of defense attorneys, who make a practice of vigorously contesting every step of the case.

Claude Drumm exercised his second peremptory challenge. A juror left the box. The clerk drew another man, and a tall, gaunt individual, with high cheekbones and lackluster eyes, came forward, held up his right hand, was sworn, and took his seat in the jury box.

"You may inquire," said Judge Markham to Perry Mason,

Perry Mason glanced over at the juror casually.

"Your name?" he said.

"George Smith," said the juror.

"You've read about this case?"

"Yes."

"Formed or expressed any opinion from what you have read?"

"No."

"You don't know anything about the facts of the case?"

"Nothing except what I've read in the papers."

"If you are selected as a juror to try this case could you fairly and truly try the defendant and render a true verdict?"

"I could."

"Will you?"

"I will."

Perry Mason slowly got to his feet. His examination of the jurors had been startlingly brief. Now he turned to this newest addition to the jury box and regarded the man frowningly.

"You understand," he said, "that you are to act as a judge of the facts, if you are selected as a juror in this case, but that, so far as the law is concerned, you will accept the law in the instructions given you by the Court?"

"I do," said the juror.

"In the event the Court should instruct you," said Perry Mason slowly and solemnly, "that under the law of this state it is incumbent upon the prosecution to prove the defendant guilty beyond all reasonable doubt, before a juror can conscientiously return a verdict of guilty, and that, therefore, it is not necessary for the defendant to take the witness stand and testify in her own behalf, but she may remain mute and rely upon the fact that the prosecution has failed to prove her guilty beyond all reasonable doubt,

148

could you and would you follow such instruction of the Court and accept it as law?"

The juror nodded his head.

"Yes," he said, "I think I could, if that's the law."

"In the event the Court should further instruct you that such a failure on the part of the defendant to take the witness stand and deny the charges made against her was not to be considered in any way by the jury in arriving at its verdict and was not to be commented upon in connection with the discussions of the case, could you and would you follow such an instruction?"

"Yes, I guess so."

Perry Mason dropped back in his chair and nodded his head casually.

"Pass for cause," he said.

Claude Drumm asked that grim question which had disqualified many of the jurors:

"Have you," he said, "any conscientious scruples against the return of a verdict which would result in the penalty of death for the defendant?"

"None," said the man.

"If you are on the jury which tries this case," said the deputy district attorney, "there would be no conscientious scruples which would prevent you returning a verdict of guilty in the event you thought the defendant had been proven guilty beyond all reasonable doubt?"

"No."

"Pass for cause," said Claude Drumm.

"The peremptory," said Judge Markham, "is with the defendant."

"Pass the peremptory," said Perry Mason.

Judge Markham nodded his head toward Claude Drumm.

"Let the jury be sworn," said the deputy district attorney.

Judge Markham addressed the jury.

"Gentlemen," he said, "arise and be sworn to try this

case. And may I congratulate counsel upon the very expeditious manner in which this jury has been selected."

The jury were sworn. Claude Drumm made an opening argument—brief, forceful and to the point. It seemed that he had stolen a leaf from the book of Perry Mason, and was determined to skip over all preliminaries, directing his attention upon one smashing blow.

"Gentlemen of the jury," he said, "I propose to show that on the night of the seventeenth of October of this year, Clinton Forbes was shot to death by the defendant in this case. I shall make no secret of the fact that the defendant had a grievance against the deceased. I shall not try to minimize that grievance. I shall put the facts entirely before you, freely, openly and frankly. I propose to show that the decedent was the husband of this defendant; that the parties had lived together in Santa Barbara until approximately a year before the date of the decedent's death; that the decedent had then surreptitiously departed without advising the defendant where he intended to go, and that the decedent took with him one Paula Cartright, the wife of a mutual friend; that the parties came to this city, where Forbes established a residence at 4889 Milpas Drive, under the name of Clinton Foley, and that Paula Cartright posed as Evelyn Foley, the wife of the deceased. I propose to show that the defendant in this case purchased a Colt automatic of thirty-eight caliber; that she devoted more than one year of her life to a careful and painstaking search, trying to locate the decedent; that shortly before the date of the murder, she located the decedent, and that she then came to this city and engaged a room in a downtown hotel, under the name of Mrs. C. M. Dangerfield.

"I expect to show that on the night of October 17th, at the hour of approximately twenty-five minutes past seven, the defendant arrived at the house occupied by her husband; that she used a skeleton key to pick the lock of that house, and entered the corridor; that she encountered her

150

husband and shot him down cold-bloodedly; that she then departed by taxicab and discharged the cab in the vicinity of the Breedmont Hotel, the hotel where she was registered under the name of Dangerfield.

"I propose to show that when she left the taxicab, she inadvertently left behind her a handkerchief. I propose to show that this handkerchief is undoubtedly the property of the defendant; that the defendant, recognizing the danger of leaving behind so deadly a clew, sought out the driver of the taxicab and had the handkerchief returned to her.

"I propose to show that the weapon which was purchased by the defendant, and for which she signed her name on the register of firearms, as kept by a sporting goods dealer in Santa Barbara, California, was the same weapon with which the deadly shots were fired. Upon this evidence I shall ask the jury to return a verdict of guilty of murder in the first degree."

During the speech, Claude Drumm did not raise his voice, but spoke with a vibrant earnestness that compelled the attention of the jurors.

When he had finished, he walked to the counsel table and sat down.

"Do you wish to make your opening address at this time, or to reserve the right?" asked Judge Markham of Perry Mason.

"We will make it later," said Perry Mason.

"Your Honor," said Drumm, getting to his feet, "it is usually a task of several days, or a day at least, to impanel a jury in a murder case. This jury has been impaneled within a very short time. I am taken somewhat by surprise. May I ask for an adjournment until tomorrow?"

Judge Markham shook his head and smiled.

"No, Counselor," he said. "The Court will proceed to hear the case. The Court happens to know that the present counsel for the defense makes a habit of expediting matters very materially. The Court feels that there is no use wasting the balance of the day."

"Very well," said Claude Drumm with calm dignity, "I shall establish the corpus delicti, by calling Thelma Benton. May it please be understood that I am calling her at this time only for the purpose of establishing the corpus delicti. I shall examine her in greater detail later on."

"Very well," said Judge Markham, "that will be the understanding."

Thelma Benton came forward, held up her hand and was sworn. She took the witness stand and testified that her name was Thelma Benton; that her age was twenty-eight; that she resided in the Riverview Apartments; that she had been acquainted with Clinton Forbes for more than three years; that she had been in his employ as a secretary in Santa Barbara, and that she was with him when he left Santa Barbara, and came with him to the residence at 4889 Milpas Drive, where she became his housekeeper.

Claude Drumm nodded.

"Did you have occasion, on the evening of October 17th of this year," he asked, "to see a dead body in the house at 4889 Milpas Drive?"

"I did."

"Whose body was that?"

"It was the body of Clinton Forbes."

"He had rented that house under the name of Clinton Foley?"

"He had."

"And who resided there with him?"

"Mrs. Paula Cartwright, who went under the name of Evelyn Foley and posed as his wife; Ah Wong, a Chinese cook, and myself."

"There was also a police dog?"

"There was."

"What was the name of the dog?"

"Prince."

"How long had Mr. Forbes owned this police dog?"

"Approximately four years."

"You had become acquainted with the dog in Santa Barbara?"

"I had."

"And the dog accompanied you to this city?"

"He did."

"And you, in turn, accompanied Mr. Forbes and Mrs. Cartright?"

"I did."

"At the time you saw the dead body of Clinton Forbes, did you also see the police dog?"

"I did."

"Where was the police dog?"

"In the same room."

"What was his condition?"

"He was dead."

"Did you notice anything which would indicate to you the manner of death?"

"Yes, the police dog had been shot, and Mr. Forbes had been shot. There was a .38 Colt automatic lying on the floor. There were also four empty cartridges on the floor of the room, where they had been ejected by the automatic mechanism of the weapon."

"When did you last see Clinton Forbes alive?"

"On the evening of October 17th."

"At approximately what hour?"

"At approximately the hour of six-fifteen o'clock in the evening."

"Were you at the house after that hour?"

"I was not. I left at that time, and Mr. Clinton Forbes was alive and well then. The next time I saw him he was dead."

"What did you notice about the condition of the body?" asked Drumm.

"You mean about the shaving?"

"Yes."

"He had evidently been shaving. There had been lather on his face, and some of it still remained. He was in the library of his house, and there was a bedroom adjoining the library, and a bathroom adjoining the bedroom."

"Where was the dog kept?"

"The dog," said Thelma Benton, "had been kept chained in the bathroom since the time when a complaint was made by a neighbor."

"I think," said Claude Drumm, "that you may cross-examine upon the matters thus far brought out in evidence."

Perry Mason nodded his head languidly. The eyes of the jurors shifted to him.

He spoke in a deeply resonant voice, but without emphasis, and in a low tone.

"The complaint was made that the dog was howling?" he asked, almost conversationally.

"Yes."

"By the next door neighbor?"

"Yes."

"And that neighbor was Mr. Arthur Cartright, the husband of the woman who was posing as the wife of Clinton Forbes?"

"Yes."

"Was Mrs. Cartright in the house at the time of the murder?"

"She was not."

"Where was she, if you know?"

"I don't know."

"When did you last see her?"

Claude Drumm was on his feet.

"Your Honor," he said, "it is obvious that this will be a part of the case of the defendant. It is improper cross-examination at this time."

"Overruled," said Judge Markham. "I will permit the question because you asked, on direct examination, about the various occupants of the house. I think the question is proper."

"Answer the question," said Perry Mason.

154

Thelma Benton raised her voice slightly and spoke rapidly.

"Paula Cartright," she said, "left the house on the morning of the 17th of October. She left behind her a note stating that . . ."

"We object," said Claude Drumm, "to the witness testifying as to the contents of the note. In the first place, it is not responsive to the question. In the second place, it is not the best evidence."

"No," said Judge Markham, "it is not the best evidence."

"Where then," asked Perry Mason, "*is* the note?"

There was a moment of awkward silence. Thelma Benton looked toward the district attorney.

"I have it," said Claude Drumm, "and intend to introduce it later on."

"I think," said Judge Markham, "the cross-examination upon this point has proceeded far enough, and that the question as to the contents of the note will not be permitted."

"Very well," said Perry Mason, "I think that is all at this time."

"Call Sam Marson," said Claude Drumm.

Sam Marson was sworn, took the witness stand, testified that his name was Sam Marson; that his age was thirty-two; that he was a taxicab driver, and had been such on the 17th of October of the present year.

"Did you see the defendant on that date?" asked Claude Drumm.

Marson leaned forward to stare at Bessie Forbes, who sat in a chair directly back of Perry Mason, flanked by a deputy sheriff.

"Yes," he said, "I seen her."

"When did you first see her?"

"About ten minutes past seven."

"Where?"

"In the vicinity of Ninth and Masonic Streets."

"What did she do?"

"She signaled me, and I pulled in to the curb. She told me she wanted to go to 4889 Milpas Drive. I took her out there and then she told me to go and ring up Parkcrest 62945 and ask for Arthur, and tell him to go over to Clint's house right away, because Clint was having a show-down with Paula."

"Very well, what did you do?" asked Claude Drumm.

"I took her there and went and telephoned, like she said, and then I came back.

"Then what happened?"

"Then she came out and I took her back to a place right near the Breedmont Hotel, and she got out."

"Did you see her again that night?"

"Yes."

"When?"

"I don't know. Near midnight, I guess. She came up to the taxicab and said that she thought she'd left the hand-kerchief in the cab. I told her she had, and gave it to her."

"She took it?"

"Yes."

"And that was the same person you had taken out to the residence at 4889 Milpas Drive?"

"Yes, that was the one."

"And you say that is the defendant in this case?"

"Yes. That's her."

Claude Drumm turned to Perry Mason.

"You may cross-examine," he said.

Perry Mason raised his voice slightly.

"The defendant left a handkerchief in your taxicab?"

"Yes."

"What did you do with it?"

"I showed it to you, and you told me to put it back."

Claude Drumm chuckled.

"Just a moment," said Perry Mason. "You don't need to bring me into this."

"Then keep yourself out of it," said Claude Drumm.

Judge Markham banged with his gavel.

"Order!" he said. "Counselor, did you wish to ask to have that answer stricken out?"

"Yes," said Perry Mason, "I move to strike it out on the ground that it is not responsive to the question."

"The motion is denied," said Judge Markham sternly. "The court believes that it was responsive to the question."

A broad smile suffused the face of the deputy district attorney.

"Did the deputy district attorney tell you what you were to testify to in this case?" asked Perry Mason.

"No, sir."

"Didn't he tell you that if I gave you the slightest opportunity, you were to testify that you had given that handkerchief to me?"

The witness squirmed uncomfortably.

Claude Drumm got to his feet with a vehement objection. Judge Markham overruled the objection, and Sam Marson said slowly, "Well, he told me that *he* couldn't ask me about what you had said to me, but that if I got a chance, it was all right to tell the jury."

"And did he also," asked Perry Mason, "tell you that when he asked you if the defendant was the person who had engaged your taxicab on the night of October 17th, you were to lean forward and look at her, so that the jury could see you were studying her features?"

"Yes, he told me to do that."

"As a matter of fact, you'd seen the defendant on several occasions prior to the time you gave your testimony. She'd been pointed out to you by the officers, and you'd seen her in the jail. You'd known for some time she was the person who engaged your taxicab on that night, isn't that right?"

"I guess so, yes."

"So that there was no necessity whatever for you to lean

forward and study the features of the defendant before you answered that question."

"Well," said Marson uncomfortably, "that's what I was told to do."

The smile had faded from Claude Drumm's face, and was replaced by a frown of irritation.

Perry Mason slowly got to his feet, stood staring for a long moment at the witness.

"Are you absolutely certain," he said, "that it was the defendant in this case who hired your taxicab?"

"Yes, sir."

"And absolutely certain that it was the defendant who came to you later on the same evening and asked you about the handkerchief?"

"Yes, sir."

"Isn't it a fact that you were not certain at the time, but that this feeling of certainty in your mind has been built up, following interviews with the authorities?"

"No, I don't think so. I knew her."

"You're certain that it was the defendant upon both occasions?"

"Yes."

"And you're certain that it was the defendant who called for the handkerchief, as you are that it was the defendant who hired you to take her out to Milpas Drive?"

"Yes, it was the same person."

Perry Mason turned abruptly and dramatically toward the back of the crowded courtroom. He flung out a hand in a swiftly dramatic gesture.

"Mae Sibley," he said, "stand up." There was a slight commotion, and then Mae Sibley stood up.

"Take a look at that person and tell me if you have ever seen her before," said Perry Mason.

Claude Drumm jumped to his feet.

"Your Honor," he said, "I object to this form of testing the recollection of the witness. It is not a proper test; nor is it proper cross-examination."

"Do you intend to connect it up, Counselor?" asked Judge Markham of Perry Mason.

"I will do better than that," said Perry Mason. "I will withdraw the question, as it was asked, and ask you, Samuel Marson, if it is not a fact that this woman who is now standing in the courtroom is not the woman who called for the handkerchief on the evening of October 17th of this year, and the woman to whom you gave the handkerchief which had been left in the taxicab?"

"No, sir," said Samuel Marson, pointing toward the defendant, "that was the woman."

"There's no chance you're mistaken?" asked Perry Mason.

"No, sir."

"And if you are mistaken as to the identity of the woman who called for the handkerchief, you might also be mistaken as to the identity of the woman who was taken by you to that house on Milpas Drive?"

"I ain't mistaken about either of 'em, but if I was mistaken on one, I could be mistaken on the other," said Marson.

Perry Mason smiled triumphantly.

"That," he said, "is all."

Claude Drumm was on his feet.

"Your Honor," he said, "may I ask for a recess until tomorrow morning?"

Judge Markham frowned and nodded his head slowly.

"Yes," he said, "the Court will adjourn until ten o'clock tomorrow morning. During the recess, the jury are admonished not to talk about the case among themselves; nor to permit it to be discussed in their presence."

Judge Markham banged his gavel, arose and stalked majestically toward his chambers in the rear of the courtroom. Perry Mason noticed Claude Drumm glance significantly at two deputies, and saw these deputies push their way through the crowd to the side of Mae Sibley. Perry Mason also pushed his way through the crowd, his

159

shoulders squared, chin outthrust. He reached the young woman's side but a few moments after the deputies had closed in on her.

"Judge Markham wants to see all three of you in his chambers," he said.

The deputies looked surprised.

"This way," said Perry Mason, and, turning, started pushing his way back toward the space within the bar.

"Oh, Drumm," he called, raising his voice.

Claude Drumm, who was about to leave the courtroom, paused.

"Would you mind stepping into the chambers of Judge Markham with me?" asked Perry Mason.

Drumm hesitated a moment, then nodded.

Together, the two attorneys entered the chambers. Behind them came the two deputies and Mae Sibley.

The Judge's chambers were lined with law books. A huge desk in the center of the room was littered with an orderly array of papers and law books that were held open. Judge Markham looked up.

"Judge," said Perry Mason, "this young woman is a witness of mine. She is under subpœna for the defense. I noticed that at a signal from the deputy district attorney, two deputies have approached her. May I ask the Court to instruct the witness that she needs to talk to no one until she is called as a witness, and to instruct the deputies that they are not to annoy her?"

Claude Drumm flushed, walked back and kicked the door shut.

"Now, then," he said, "since you've brought this subject up, and since court isn't in session, we'll settle it right here and now."

Perry Mason glared at him belligerently.

"All right," he said, "go ahead and settle it."

"What I intended to do," said Claude Drumm, "was to find out from this young woman if she had been paid to impersonate the defendant. I wanted to find out if an arrangement had been made with her to approach this taxi-cab driver and claim that she was the person who had hired the taxicab earlier in the day, and who had left a handkerchief in the cab."

"All right," said Perry Mason, "suppose she said yes to all of that; *then* what did you intend to do?"

"I intended to discover the identity of the person who had paid her to make such false representations and to get a warrant for his arrest," said Claude Drumm.

"All right," said Perry Mason in an ominous drawl, "I'm the person. I did it. What are you going to do about it?"

"Gentlemen," said Judge Markham, "it seems to me this discussion is getting somewhat beyond the subject."

"Not a bit of it," said Mason. "I knew this was coming and I want to have it settled right here and now. There's no law against a woman impersonating another. It's no crime to claim to be the owner of lost property, unless the claim is made for the purpose of obtaining the possession of that lost property."

"That was exactly the purpose of this deception," shouted Claude Drumm.

Perry Mason smiled.

"You'll remember, Drumm," he said, "that I rang up the authorities and turned the handkerchief over to them, just as soon as it had been given to me, and that Miss Sibley gave it to me just as soon as she received it from the taxi driver. What I was doing was testing the recollection of the taxi driver. I knew blamed well that by the time you got done coaching him, he'd be so positive of the identity of the defendant, that no amount of cross-examination would shake him. I cross-examined him first, and by an object lesson, rather than by questions, that's all. I was within my rights."

Judge Markham looked at Perry Mason, and there was a twinkle in his eyes.

"Well," he said, "the Court isn't called upon at this

time to pass upon the ethics of the question, and it isn't called upon to pass upon the question of whether there was a larceny of a handkerchief. The Court is only called upon to pass upon your request, Counselor, that your witnesses be allowed to give their testimony in court, and that the officers do not seek to intimidate them."

"That's all I want," said Perry Mason, but his eyes remained fastened on Claude Drumm. "I know what I'm doing, and I'm responsible for what I do, and I don't want any woman terrified by a lot of bullies."

"What you've done will get you before the grievance committee of the Bar Association!" shouted Claude Drumm.

"That's fine," Perry Mason told him. "I'll be only too glad to discuss the matter with you there. But in the meantime, you keep your hands off my witnesses."

"Gentlemen, gentlemen," snapped Judge Markham, getting to his feet. "I'm going to insist upon order. Counselor Mason has presented a request. You should know, Mr. Drumm, that the request is in order. If this person is a witness subpœnaed by the defense, you will refrain from seeking to intimidate her."

Claude Drumm gulped and colored visibly.

"Very well," he said.

"This way," said Perry Mason, smiling, and taking Mae Sibley's arm, took her from the chambers.

As he opened the door into the courtroom, there was a vivid flash of light, a sudden "*poof.*"

The girl screamed and covered her face.

"Don't get excited," Perry Mason told her. "It's just newspaper photographers taking your picture."

Claude Drumm pushed his way to Mason's side. His face was white, his eyes blazing.

"You deliberately engineered that whole thing!" he said. "Just to get a dramatic story on the front page of the newspapers!"

Perry Mason grinned at him.

"Any objections?" he asked.

"Lots of them!" blazed Claude Drumm.

"All right," said Perry Mason slowly and ominously, "be damn careful how you make 'em."

For a long moment the two men glared at each other, Claude Drumm, white with fury, but impotent against the rugged strength of the criminal lawyer, stared into the steady eyes and knew that he was licked. Still white with fury, he turned on his heel and walked away.

Perry Mason turned to Mae Sibley.

"I didn't want you talking to the deputies," he said, "but there's no reason why you can't talk with the newspaper reporters."

"What shall I tell them?" she asked.

"Tell them anything you know," he said, and lifted his hat as he walked away. From the door of the courtroom, he looked behind him.

Half a dozen newspaper reporters eagerly surrounded Mae Sibley, and were asking frantic questions.

Still smiling, Perry Mason pushed his way through the swinging door, out into the corridor.

CHAPTER XVIII

PERRY MASON looked at his watch when he entered his office. It was a cold, blustery night outside, and the radiators were hissing comfortably. The hour was exactly eight forty-five.

Perry Mason switched on the lights and set a leather case on Della Street's desk. He snapped a catch, took off a cover, and disclosed a portable typewriter. He reached in his overcoat pocket, took out a pair of gloves and put them on. From a brief-case he took several sheets of paper and a stamped envelope. He had just placed them on the desk when Della Street came in.

"Did you see the papers?" she asked, as she closed the door and slipped out of her fur coat.

"Yes," said Perry Mason, and grinned.

"Tell me," she said, "did you arrange that whole business so you'd have a dramatic punch for the close of the trial?"

"Sure," he told her. "Why not?"

"Weren't you coming pretty close to a violation of the law? Can't they make trouble for you before the grievance committee?"

"I doubt it," he said. "It was legitimate cross-examination."

"How do you mean—cross-examination?" she asked.

"It would have been perfectly permissible for me to have stood several women in line and asked Sam Marson to pick out the one who had left the handkerchief in his taxicab. It would have been perfectly permissible for me to have pointed to one of the women and told him that I thought that was the one. It would have been perfectly permissible for me to have taken one woman to him and asked him if he wasn't certain that that was the one, or to have told him that it was the one."

"Well?" she asked.

"Well," he said, "I only went one step farther. I found out that he was uncertain about the identity of the woman. I capitalized on that uncertainty, that's all. I took a woman, dressed her approximately the same as Mrs. Forbes had been dressed, put the same kind of perfume on her, and had her tell the taxi driver that she had left the handkerchief in his cab. Naturally, he didn't question her word, because he was uncertain in his recollection of the woman who *had* left the handkerchief in his cab.

"I knew that by the time the authorities got done with him, he'd make a positive identification. That's a slick way they have of taking a witness over a period of time, and letting him become more and more positive. They showed him Bessie Forbes, on at least a dozen different occasions. They did it casually, so that he didn't know he was being hypnotized. First, they showed him the woman, and told him that was the one who had been in his cab. Then they brought him in and confronted her with him, and told her that he had identified her. She didn't say anything, but refused to answer questions. That made Marson a little more certain. Bit by bit, they built him up in his testimony, and coached him, until he was so positive in his own mind, there couldn't be any doubt whatever. It's the way the prosecution prepares all cases. They naturally make witnesses more strong in their identifications."

"I know," she said, "but how about the handkerchief?"

"In order to be larceny," he said, "there has got to be an intent to steal. There wasn't any intent to steal. The woman was getting the handkerchief for me. I was getting it for the authorities. I turned it over to them sooner than they would have found it otherwise, and gave them the information."

She frowned and shook her head.

"Perhaps," she said, "but you certainly pulled a fast one."

"Of course I pulled a fast one," he told her. "It's what I'm paid for. I simply cross-examined him in an unorthodox manner, and cross-examined him before the district attorney had an opportunity to poison his mind with a lot of propaganda, that's all . . . don't take off your gloves, Della; leave them on."

"Why?" she asked, regarding the long black gloves on her hands and arms.

"Because," he said, "we're going to pull another fast one, and I don't want either one of us to leave fingerprints on the paper.

She stared at him for a minute, and then said: "Is it within the law?"

"I think it is," he told her, "but we're not going to get caught."

He walked over to the door and locked it.

"Take a sheet of this paper," he said, "and put it in that portable typewriter."

"I don't like portables," she told him. "I'm used to my office machine."

"That's all right," he told her. "Typewriters are as individual as handwriting. A handwriting expert can tell the kind of a typewriter a document was written on, and can also identify the typewriter, itself, if he has access to it and a chance to compare the writing."

"This is a new portable," she said.

"Exactly," he told her, "and I'm going to put some of the type a little out of line, so it won't look quite so new."

He went to the machine and started bending the type bars.

"What's the idea?" she asked.

"We're going to write a confession."

"What sort of a confession?"

"A confession," he said, "to the murder of Paula Cartright."

She stared at him with wide, startled eyes.

"Good heavens!" she said, "and then what are you going to do with the confession?"

"We're going to mail it," he said, "to the city editor of *The Chronicle*."

She remained motionless, staring at him with apprehensive eyes, then suddenly took a deep breath, walked over to her chair, sat down and slid some of the sheets of paper into the portable typewriter.

"Afraid, Della?" he asked.

"No," she said. "If you tell me to do it, I'm going to do it."

"I think it's skating on pretty thin ice," he told her, "but I think I can get you out if anything happens."

"That's all okay," she said. "I'd do anything for you. Go ahead and tell me what you want written."

"I'm going to dictate this," he said slowly, "and you can take it directly on the typewriter."

He moved to her shoulder and said in a low voice, "Write this, addressed to the city editor of *The Chronicle*.

"DEAR SIR:

"I notice that in your paper you printed an interview with Elizabeth Walker, in which she said that I had made statements on several occasions that I intended to die on the scaffold; that I spent most of my time staring through binoculars at the residence occupied by Clinton Forbes, who was then going under the name of Clinton Foley.

"All of these things are correct.

"I notice that you have published an editorial demanding that the authorities apprehend me, and also apprehend Paula Cartright, my wife, before the trial of Bessie Forbes is allowed to proceed, the intimation being that I killed Clinton Forbes.

"This accusation is unjust and untrue.

"I did not kill Clinton Forbes; but I did kill my wife, Paula Cartright.

"Under the circumstances, I think that the public is entitled to know exactly what happened."

Perry Mason paused until the clicking of the typewriter signified that Della Street had caught up with him. Then he waited until she raised her eyes to his.

"Getting frightened, Della?" he asked.

"No," she said. "Go on."

"It's loaded with dynamite," he told her.

"It's oke with me," she said. "If you can take a chance, so can I."

"All right," he said, "go on from there:

"I lived in Santa Barbara with my wife, and I was happy. I was friendly with Clinton Forbes, and his wife. I knew that Clinton Forbes was a rotter, so far as any moral sense was concerned, but I liked him. I knew that he was playing around with half a dozen women. I never had any suspicion that my wife was one of them. Abruptly, and out of a clear sky, I realized the truth. I was a ruined man. My happiness was wrecked and so was my home. I determined to hunt down Clinton Forbes and kill him, as I would a dog.

"It took me ten months to find him. Then I found him living on Milpas Drive, under the name of Clinton Foley. I found that the adjoining house was for rent, furnished, and I moved in, purposely engaged a housekeeper who was stone deaf, and who could not, therefore, engage in neighborhood gossip. Before I killed Clinton Foley, I wanted to find out something about his habits. I wanted to find out something about how he was treating Paula, and whether she was happy. To that end, I spent most of my time studying the house through binoculars.

"It was a slow and tedious undertaking. On occasions, I would see intimate glimpses of the home life of the man on whom I spied. At other times, days would go past, during which I would see nothing. In the end, I satisfied myself that Paula was desperately unhappy.

"And yet, despite all of my plans, I failed in my purpose. I waited until there was a dark night that suited my intentions, and sneaked across the grounds to the house of my enemy. I fully intended to kill him and claim my wife. I gave my housekeeper a letter to my lawyer. In that letter I enclosed my will. In case anything happened to me, I wanted to know that my affairs had been put in order.

"I found the back door of the house unlocked. Clinton Foley had a police dog, Prince, who acted as watch dog, but Prince knew me, because I had been friendly with Clinton Forbes in Santa Barbara. In place of barking at me, the dog was glad to see me. He jumped on me and licked my hand. I patted his head and walked quietly through the back of the house. I was going through the library, when I suddenly encountered my wife. She stared at me and screamed. I grabbed her and threatened to choke her if she didn't keep quiet.

"She almost fainted with terror. I made her sit down, and talked with her. She told me that Clinton Forbes and his housekeeper, Thelma Benton, had been carrying on a clandestine affair for years; that the affair had dated back even before his affair with her; that Forbes had gone out with Thelma Benton, and that she was alone in the house; that Ah Wong, the cook, had gone out to spend the evening with some Chinese friends, as was his custom.

"I told her that I intended to kill Forbes, and that I wanted her to go away with me. She told me that I must do nothing of the sort, and that she had ceased to love me and could never be happy with me. She threatened to call the police and tell them about what I intended to do. She started for the telephone. I struggled with her and she started to scream. I choked her.

"I can never explain the emotions of that moment. I loved her passionately. I knew that she no longer loved me. She was struggling with me, to save the man who had betrayed me and whom I hated. I became insensible to my surroundings. I only knew that I was crushing her neck in a frantic grip. When I regained my senses sufficiently to realize what I was doing, she was dead. I had choked her to death.

"Clinton Forbes was building an addition to his garage. The cement work was in. The floor was about to be laid. I went into the garage and found a pick and shovel. I dug up the ground where the floor was to be poured, buried the body of my wife in a shallow grave, took the extra dirt in a wheelbarrow, carried it to the rear of the lot and dumped it. I wanted to wait for Clinton Forbes, but I dared not do so. The thing which I had done had completely unnerved me. I was trembling like a leaf. I realized that my temper had betrayed me into killing the woman I loved. I realized, however, that I was safe from discovery. The contractors were about to pour the cement floor in the addition to the garage, and that would cover up the evidences of my crime. I went to another section of town, rented a room under an assumed name, built up a second identity for myself, and have been living there ever since.

"I am making this confession because I feel that it is only fair that I do so. I killed my wife. I did not kill Clinton Forbes—I only wish that I had. He deserved to die, but I did not kill him.

"I am safe from detection. No one will ever penetrate the secret of my present disguise.

"Very truly yours,"

Perry Mason waited until the girl had finished her typing, then he took the paper from the portable machine, and read it over carefully.

"That," he said, "will be all right."

She looked at him with white, drawn features and staring eyes.

"What are you going to do with it?" she asked.

"I am going to take the will of Arthur Cartright as a pattern," he said, "and forge his signature to this document."

She stared at him for a moment silently, then walked across the office to a table on which was pen and ink, dipped a pen in the inkwell, and handed it to him. Wordlessly, she walked over to the safe, spun the dials, opened the doors of the safe, took out the will of Arthur Cartright and handed it to him.

In purposeful silence, Perry Mason sat down at the table, made several practice signatures on a piece of paper, then laboriously forged the signature of Arthur Cartright to the confession. He folded the paper, then handed Della Street the stamped envelope.

"Address that," he said, "to the city editor of *The Chronicle*."

He put the cover back on the portable typewriter.

"What are you going to do now?" she asked.

"Mail the letter," he said, "and see that this portable

typewriter is placed where the authorities will never find it, take a taxicab and go home."

She looked at him steadily for a moment, then walked to the door.

She paused, with her hand on the knob, stood motionless for a moment, then turned and came back to him.

"Chief," she said, "I wish you wouldn't do it."

"Do what?"

"Take these chances."

"I have to do it," he said.

"It isn't right," she said.

"It is if the results are right."

"What results are you trying to get?"

"I want," he said, "the cement floor in that garage extension broken up, and the place underneath carefully searched."

"Then why not go to the authorities and ask them to do it?"

He laughed sarcastically.

"A fat chance that they'd do anything," he said. "They hate my guts. They are trying to get Bessie Forbes convicted. They wouldn't do anything that would weaken their case in front of a jury. Their theory is that she's guilty, and that's all there is to it. They won't listen to anything else, and if I ask them to do anything, they'd naturally think that I was trying to slip over a fast one."

"What will happen when you send this to *The Chronicle?*" she asked.

"It's a cinch," he said. "They'll smash up that floor."

"How will they do it?"

"They'll just do it, that's all."

"Will they get permisson from anybody?"

"Don't be silly," he told her. "Forbes bought the place and owns it. He's dead. Bessie Forbes is his wife. If she's acquitted of this murder, she'll inherit his property."

"If she isn't?" asked Della Street.

"She's going to be," he told her grimly.

"What makes you think there's a body under there?" she asked.

"Listen," he told her, "let's look at this thing from a reasonable standpoint and quit being stampeded by a lot of facts that don't mean anything. You remember when Arthur Cartright first came to us?"

"Yes, of course."

"You remember what he said? He wanted a will made. He wanted a will made so that the property would be taken by the woman who was at present living as the wife of Clinton Foley, in the house on Milpas Drive."

"Yes."

"All right. Then he made a will and sent it to me, and the will didn't read that way."

"Why didn't it?" she asked.

"Because," he said, "he knew that there was no use leaving his property to a woman who was already dead. In some way he'd found out that she was dead."

"Then he didn't murder her?"

"I'm not saying that, but I don't think he did."

"But isn't it a crime to forge a confession of this sort?"

"Under certain circumstances, it may be," Perry Mason said.

"I can't see under what circumstances it wouldn't be," she told him.

"We'll cross that bridge when we come to it."

"And you think that Arthur Cartright knew that his wife was dead?"

"Yes, he'd been devoted to her. He'd been searching for her for ten months. He'd been living next door to her for two months, spying on the man he hated, and trying to find out if his wife was happy. He made up his mind he was going to kill Clinton Forbes. He felt that he would be executed for that murder. He wanted his property to go to his wife; not to Forbes' wife, but to Paula Cartright, but he didn't care to make his will in favor of Paula Cartright before he had committed the murder, because he thought that would bring an investigation. So he made his will, or wanted to make his will, so that it would transfer the property to the woman, under the name of Evelyn Foley.

"You can see what he had in mind. He wanted to hush up any scandal. He intended to kill Foley and to plead guilty to murder and be executed. He wanted his will made so that his property would go to the woman who was apparently the widow of the man he had murdered, and he wanted to do it in such a way that no questions would be asked, and her real identity would never be known. He did that to spare her the disgrace of having the various facts become public."

She stood perfectly still, her eyes staring down at the tips of her shoes.

"Yes," she said, "I think I understand."

"And then," said Perry Mason, "something happened, so that Arthur Cartright changed his mind. He knew that there was no use leaving the property to his wife, Paula. He wanted to leave it to some one because he didn't expect to remain alive. He had undoubtedly been in touch with Bessie Forbes, and knew that she was in the city, so he left the property to her."

"What makes you say he had been in touch with Bessie Forbes?" asked Della Street.

"Because the taxi driver says that Bessie Forbes told him to telephone Parkcrest 62945, which was Cartright's number, and tell Arthur to go next door to Clint's place. That shows that she knew where Cartright was, and that Cartright knew that she knew."

"I see," said Della Street, and was silent for several seconds.

"Are you certain," asked Della Street, "that Mrs. Cartright didn't run away with Arthur Cartright and leave Clinton Forbes, just as she had left Cartright in Santa Barbara?"

"Yes," he said, "I'm virtually certain."

"What makes you so certain?"

"The note," he said, "that was left wasn't in the handwriting of Paula Cartright."

"You're certain about that?"

"Virtually," he said. "It's approximately the same handwriting as that which appeared on the telegraph blank that was sent from Midwick. I've had samples of Mrs. Cartright's handwriting sent from Santa Barbara, and the two don't check."

"Does the district attorney's office know that?" she asked.

"I don't think so," he told her.

Della Street stared at Perry Mason thoughtfully.

"Was it Thelma Benton's handwriting?" she asked.

"I've had several specimens of Thelma Benton's handwriting, and those specimens seem entirely different from the handwriting of the note and the telegraph blank."

"Mrs. Forbes?" she asked.

"No, it isn't her handwriting. I had Mrs. Forbes write me a letter from the jail."

"There's an editorial in *The Chronicle*," she said, "did you see it?"

"No," he said. "What is it?"

"It states that in view of the dramatic surprise that impeaches the testimony of the taxicab driver, it is your solemn duty to put your client on the stand and let her explain her connection with the case. The editor says that this air of mystery is all right for a hardened criminal who is being tried for a crime of which every one knows he is guilty, and who desires to assert his constitutional rights, but not for a woman like Mrs. Forbes.

"I didn't see the editorial," said Perry Mason.

"Will it make any difference in your plans?"

"Certainly not," he told her. "I'm trying this case. I'm exercising my judgment for the best interests of my client; not the judgment of some newspaper editor."

"All of the evening papers," she said, "comment upon

the consummate skill with which you manipulated things so that the dénouement came as a dramatic finale to the day's trial, and managed to impeach the testimony of the taxi driver before the prosecution had even built up its case."

"It wasn't any particular skill on my part," Perry Mason said. "Claude Drumm walked into it. He started to strong-arm my witness. I wouldn't stand for it. I grabbed her and took her into the judge's chambers to make a protest. I knew that Drumm was going to claim I'd been guilty of unprofessional conduct, and I wanted to have it out with him right then and there."

"What did Judge Markham think?" she asked.

"I don't know," he told her, "and I don't give a damn. I know what my rights are and I stood on them. I'm fighting to protect a client."

Abruptly she came to him, put her hand on his shoulders.

"Chief," she said, "I doubted you once. I just want you to know that I'll never do it again. I'm for you, right or wrong."

He smiled, patted her on the shoulder.

"All right," he said, "take a taxi and go home. If anybody should want me, you don't know where to find me."

She nodded, walked to the door, and this time went out without hesitating.

Perry Mason waited until she had gone down in the elevator. Then he switched out the lights, put on his overcoat, sealed the letter, took the portable typewriter and went to his car. He drove to another part of the city, posted the letter in a mail box, and then took a winding road which led to a reservoir in the hills back of the city. He drove along the bank of the reservoir, slowed his car, took the portable typewriter and flung it into the reservoir. By the time the water splashed up in a miniature geyser, Perry Mason was stepping on the throttle of his automobile.

CHAPTER XIX

Rᴀᴅɪᴀᴛᴏʀs were still hissing comfortably in the building when Perry Mason sat down with Paul Drake.

"Paul," he said, "I want a man who's willing to take a chance."

"I've got lots of them," Drake said. "What do you want?"

"I want this man to call up Thelma Benton, say that he's a reporter of *The Chronicle*; that the city editor has given an okay to pay ten thousand dollars for exclusive rights to publish her diary if it's as represented.

"I want him to make an appointment to meet Thelma Benton where he can inspect the diary. She may, or may not, have some one with her. I doubt if she'll surrender the diary for inspection. But she'll let him look at it.

"I want that man to turn to the date that's marked October 18th, and tear the leaf from the book."

"What's on that leaf that you want?" asked the detective.

"I don't know."

"She'll make a holler."

"Naturally."

"What can they do to the man who does that?"

"Not very much," Perry Mason said. "They may try to throw a scare into him, but that's about all they can do."

"Couldn't she sue for damages if the thing was made public?"

"I'm not going to make it public," he said. "I'm simply going to let her know that I have it."

"Look here," Drake said, "it's none of my business, and you certainly don't need me to tell you how to practice law, but you're skating on damned thin ice. I've told you that before, and I'm telling it to you again."

"I know I'm skating on thin ice," Perry Mason said

morosely, "but there's nothing they can get me for. I claim that I'm within my rights on everything I've done. Newspapers do things twice as bad as that every day in the week and nobody says anything to them."

"You're not a newspaper," Drake pointed out.

"I know I'm not," said Mason. "But I'm a lawyer and I'm representing a client who is entitled to a fair trial. By God, I'm going to see that she gets it!"

"Does all this spectacular and dramatic stuff constitute your idea of a fair trial?"

"Yes. My idea of a fair trial is to bring out the facts. I'm going to bring out the facts."

"All of the facts, or just the facts that are favorable to your client?"

"Well," said Perry Mason, grinning, "I'm not going to try the case for the district attorney, if that's what you mean; that's up to him."

Paul Drake scraped back his chair.

"You'll defend us if we get into a jam over this?" he asked.

"Certainly," Perry Mason told him. "I wouldn't get you into anything that I wouldn't go into myself."

"The trouble with you," the detective told him, "is that you go into too darn much. Incidentally, you're getting the reputation of being a legal wizard."

"How do you mean—a wizard?" Mason asked.

"They figure that you can pull a verdict out of the hat, just like a magician pulls out a rabbit," Drake told him. "Your methods aren't orthodox; they're dramatic and effective."

"We're a dramatic people," Perry Mason said slowly. "We're not like the English. The English want dignity and order. We want the dramatic and the spectacular. It's a national craving. We're geared to a rapid rate of thought. We want to have things move in a spectacular manner."

"Well, that's the way you do it, all right," Drake said,

getting to his feet. "That stunt this afternoon was certainly clever. You've got every newspaper in town featuring, not the case against Bessie Forbes, but the spectacular manner in which the testimony of the taxi driver was virtually discredited. Every newspaper in the city acts on the assumption that the entire testimony of the cab driver is valueless."

"Well, it is," said Perry Mason.

"And yet," Drake told him thoughtfully, "you know as well as I do that Bessie Forbes actually went out there in that taxicab. She was the woman who went to the house."

"That," said the lawyer, "is a matter of conjecture and speculation unless the district attorney introduces some evidence to prove it."

"Where's he going to get the evidence from, now that his cab driver has been discredited?"

"That," Perry Mason assured him, "is something for the district attorney to worry about."

"All right," Drake told him, "I'm on my way. Is there anything else you want?"

"I think," said Perry Mason slowly, "that will be all for a while."

"God knows, it's enough!" said Paul Drake slowly, and walked out of the office.

Perry Mason tilted back in his swivel chair and closed his eyes. He remained motionless, save for the tips of his fingers, which drummed gently upon the arms of his chair. He was sitting in that position when a key sounded in the lock of the outer door, and Frank Everly entered the office.

Frank Everly was the law clerk who looked up routine legal matters for Perry Mason, and sat with him in the trial of cases. He was young, eager, ambitious, and filled with a boundless enthusiasm.

"Can I talk with you, Chief?" he asked.

Perry Mason opened his eyes and frowned.

"Yes," he said, "come in. What is it you want?"

Frank Everly sat down on the edge of the chair and seemed ill at ease.

"Go on," said Perry Mason. "What is it?"

"I wanted to ask you," said Frank Everly, "as a personal favor, to put Bessie Forbes on the witness stand."

"What's the idea?" asked Mason curiously.

"I have been listening to a lot of talk," said Everly. "Not ordinary gossip, you understand, but the talk of lawyers, of judges and newspaper men."

Mason smiled patiently.

"All right, Everly, what did you hear?"

"If you don't put that woman on the witness stand, and she's convicted, it's going to mean that your reputation will be ruined," he said.

"All right," Perry Mason told him; "it'll be ruined then."

"But don't you see?" said Everly. "She's innocent. Everybody knows that she's innocent, now. The case against her is founded entirely on circumstantial evidence. All that it needs is a denial from her and an explanation, and the jury will render a verdict of not guilty as a matter of course."

"You really feel that way about it?" asked Perry Mason curiously.

"Of course I feel that way about it."

"And you think it's a shame I won't let her get on the stand and tell her story?"

"I think it's a responsibility that you've no right to take, sir," said Everly. "Please don't misunderstand me, but I'm talking to you as one attorney to another. You have a duty to your client; a duty to your profession; and a duty to yourself."

"Suppose she gets on the stand, tells her story, and *then* is convicted?" said Perry Mason.

"But she couldn't be," said Everly. "Everybody sympathizes with her, and now that the evidence of the taxi driver has blown up, there's nothing to it."

Perry Mason stared at the clerk steadily.

"Frank," he said, "I don't know anything that has cheered me up as much as this talk with you."

"You mean you're going to put her on the stand?"

"No, I mean I'm *not* going to put her on the stand; not under any circumstances."

"Why?" asked Frank Everly.

"Because," said Perry Mason slowly, "you think she's innocent now. Everybody thinks she's innocent. That means the jury thinks she's innocent. If I put her on the witness stand I can't make the jury think she's any more innocent. If I don't put her on, they may think she's got a dumb lawyer, but they'll return a verdict of not guilty.

"Now, I'm going to tell you something, young man. There are lots of ways of trying a lawsuit. There's the slow, tedious way, indulged in by lawyers who haven't any particular plan of campaign, other than to walk into court and snarl over objections, haggle over technicalities, and drag the facts out so interminably that no one knows just what it's all about. Then there's the dramatic method of trying a lawsuit. That's the method I try to follow.

"Somewhere along the line the district attorney is going to rest his case. I'm going to try and stampede the situation so that when the district attorney rests his case the sympathies of the jury are all going to be with the defendant. Then I'm going to throw the case right into the lap of the jury right then. They'll return a verdict, without even stopping to think it over, if it goes right."

"What if it doesn't go right?" asked Everly.

"If it doesn't go right," said Perry Mason, "I'll probably lose my reputation as a trial lawyer."

"But you've got no right to jeopardize that," said Frank Everly.

"The hell I haven't," Perry Mason told him. "I've got no right not to."

He got to his feet and switched out the lights.

"Come on, son," he said, "let's go home."

CHAPTER XX

CLAUDE DRUMM opened his morning attack, showing only too plainly his resentment of the dramatic defeat of the previous day. His manner was cold, formal and savage. He went ahead grimly with the gory details of impressing upon the jurors the fact that a murder had been committed; a murder, if you please, where a man's house had been invaded; where the man had been shot down in cold blood while in the act of shaving.

Witness after witness was called to the stand, examined with short, crisp questions, and each witness added his bit to the feeling of horror which permeated the courtroom.

These witnesses were the police officers who had come upon the scene. They described what they had found in the room. They told of the position of the body; of the faithful watchdog who had been ruthlessly shot down while trying to protect his master.

A police photographer produced a complete file of prints showing the house, the rooms, the body lying grim and grotesque on the floor of the sumptuous room. There was even a close-up of the head of the police dog, showing the glassy eyes, the lolling tongue, and the inevitable dark pool which seeped out from the body.

There was the autopsy surgeon who testified in great technical detail as to the course of the bullets; the distance from which they were fired, as evidenced by the powder burns on the skin of the deceased, and the singed hair of the dog.

From time to time, Perry Mason ventured some diffident cross-examination—questions asked in a meek tone of voice, designed to bring out some fact which the witness had overlooked, or to explain some statement which the witness had made. There was none of the battle of wits which the spectators had expected to see; none of that flashing brilliance which characterized the dramatic criminal lawyer.

The spectators had assembled in large numbers to see a show. They came in with expectant smiles upon their faces. They looked at Perry Mason, nudged one another and pointed out the great criminal lawyer—each to his neighbor.

Slowly, the expectant smiles faded from their faces. There came frowns, lowering glances at the defendant. This was a grim business—this was murder. And some one should pay for it.

The jurors had taken their places in the morning with cordial nods for Perry Mason; with tolerant glances toward the defendant. By noon, they were avoiding the eyes of Perry Mason; were leaning forward to get the gruesome details from the lips of the witnesses.

Frank Everly had lunch with Perry Mason, and it was evident that Everly labored under some great emotion. He barely tasted his soup, nibbled at his meat, refused his dessert.

"May I say something, sir?" he asked when Perry Mason had settled back in the chair, a cigarette between his lips.

Perry Mason regarded him with patient, tolerant eyes.

"Certainly," he said.

"This case is slipping through your fingers," blurted Frank Everly.

"Yes?" asked Perry Mason.

"I've heard comments in the courtroom. This morning you could have got the woman off without any difficulty. Now she'll never be able to save herself—not unless she can prove an alibi. That jury is commencing to realize the horror of the situation; the fact that it was a cold-blooded murder. Think of the argument Drumm is going to make about the loyal watchdog who gave his life to save his master. When the surgeon brought out the fact that the

182

gun was within but a few inches of the dog's chest when it was fired; was within less than two feet of Clinton Forbes when he was killed, I could see the jurors look at each other significantly."

Perry Mason was undisturbed.

"Yes," he said, "that's pretty telling evidence, and the worst blow is going to come out this afternoon, right after the trial starts."

"How do you mean?" asked Frank Everly.

"Unless I'm badly mistaken," said Perry Mason, "the first witness after lunch will be the man who's been brought from Santa Barbara, who has the firearm register. He'll show the registration of the gun that did the killing; show when it was received; when it was sold, and identify Mrs. Forbes as the one to whom the gun was sold. Then he'll bring the gun register into evidence and show her signature. That fact, coming on top of the morning's evidence, will alienate every bit of sympathy from the defendant."

"But can't you stop it in some way?" asked Everly. "You could keep making objections; keep the limelight on yourself; keep it from seeming to be so frightfully horrid."

Perry Mason puffed placidly on his cigarette.

"I don't want to stop it," he said.

"But you could make a break. You could do something that would keep the horror from cumulating in the minds of the jurors."

"That's just what I want to do," said Perry Mason.

"For heaven's sake, why?" asked Frank Everly.

Perry Mason smiled.

"Did you ever run for a political office?" he asked.

"No, of course not," said the young man.

"If you had," said Perry Mason, "you'd realize what a fickle thing the mass mind is."

"What do you mean by that?"

"Simply that there's no loyalty in it; no consistency in

it," said Perry Mason. "And a jury is a manifestation of a mass mind."

"I don't see what you're driving at," the clerk said.

"On the other hand," said Perry Mason, "you've doubtless been to a good show."

"Why, yes, of course."

"You've been to shows where there's been some strong emotional scene; where there's been something that's brought tears to your eyes, a lump to your throat?"

"Yes," said Everly dubiously, "I have, but I don't see what that's got to do with it."

"Try and remember back to the last show you went to that was like that," Perry Mason said, watching the smoke curl upward from the end of his cigarette.

"Yes, I saw one just a few nights ago," Everly said.

"Now, then, can you remember the most dramatic part of the show—the place where the lump in your throat was biggest—where your eyes felt moist?"

"Certainly, I doubt if I'll ever forget it. It was a scene where the woman . . ."

"Never mind that right now," interrupted Perry Mason. "But let me ask you: what were you doing three minutes after that emotional scene?"

Everly looked at him in surprise.

"Why, sitting right there in the theater, of course."

"No, I don't mean that," Perry Mason said. "What was your emotion?"

"Why," said Everly, "I was just watching the play and . . ." Abruptly he smiled.

"Now," said Perry Mason, "I think you're getting my point. What were you doing?"

"I was laughing," said Everly.

"Exactly," Perry Mason said, as though that disposed of the matter.

Everly watched him in puzzled bewilderment for a few moments.

"But," he said, "I don't see what that's got to do with the jury in this case."

"It has everything to do with it," Perry Mason said. "A jury is an audience. It's a small audience, but it's an audience just the same. Now, the playwrights who are successful with plays have to know human nature. They recognize the fickleness of the mass mind. They know that it's incapable of loyalty; that it's incapable of holding any emotion for any great period of time. If there hadn't been a chance to laugh after that dramatic scene in the play you saw, the play would have been a flop.

"That audience was fickle, just like all audiences are fickle. They had gone through an emotional strain of sympathizing with the heroine in her darkest hour. They felt for her. That feeling was sincere. They would have died to have saved her. They would have killed the villain, could they have laid hands on him. They felt honestly, sincerely and wholeheartedly. *But* they couldn't have held the emotion for more than three minutes, to have saved their lives. It wasn't their trouble; it was the heroine's trouble. Having felt for her deeply and sincerely, they wanted to even the emotional scales by laughing. The wise playwright knew that. He gave them an excuse to laugh. And, if you'd studied psychology, you'd have noticed how eagerly the audience grasped at that opportunity to laugh."

Everly's eyes lit up.

"All right," he said, "now tell me just how that applies to the jury. I'm commencing to think I see."

"This case," Perry Mason said, "is going to be short, snappy and dramatic. The policy of the district attorney is to emphasize the horror of a murder case; to emphasize the fact that it's not a battle of wits between counsel, but the bringing to justice of a human fiend who has killed. Ordinarily, the defense attorney tries to keep that impression of horror from creeping into the case. He jumps to his feet with objections to photographs. He waves his arms

185

and shouts arguments. He crouches in front of the witnesses and points his finger in dramatic cross-examination. It has a tendency to break the emotional chain; to soften the horror of the situation, and to draw the jurors back to the courtroom drama, instead of letting their minds revert to the horror of the murder."

"Well," said Frank Everly, "I should think that would be exactly what you'd want to do in this case."

"No," said Perry Mason slowly, "it always pays to do exactly the opposite of what custom decrees. That is particularly true with Claude Drumm. Claude Drumm is a logical fighter; a dangerous, dogged adversary, but he has no subtlety about him. He has no sense of relative values. He isn't intuitive. He can't 'feel' the mental state of a jury. He's accustomed to putting in all of this stuff after a long battle; after the attorney on the other side has done everything possible to soften the horror of the situation.

"Did you ever see two men in a tug of war, where one man let go suddenly and the other man staggered backwards off balance and fell down?"

"Yes, of course."

"For the simple reason," said Perry Mason, "that he was pulling too hard. He was expecting a continued opposition. When he didn't get it, he pulled so hard that he was thrown down by the very vehemence of his own effort."

"I think I begin to see," Frank Everly said.

"Exactly," Perry Mason told him. "The jurors came into court this morning, interested spectators expecting to see a show. Drumm started in showing them horrors. I didn't do anything about it, and Claude Drumm simply went wild on the horror angle. He's had the jurors soaked in horror all the morning. He'll continue to soak them in horror after lunch. Unconsciously the minds of the jurors will seek some relief. They'll want something to laugh at. They'll unconsciously pray for something dramatic, such as happened yesterday, to take their minds away from the horror. It's a subconscious effort of the mind to adjust itself. Having experienced too much horror, it wants a bit of laughter as an antidote. It's part of the fickleness of the human mind.

"And remember this, Frank: whenever you get to the trial of a case, never try to arouse one single emotion in the minds of a jury and bear down steadily on that emotion.

"Pick some dominant emotion if you want, but touch on it only for a few moments. Then swing your argument to something else. Then come back to it. The human mind is like a pendulum: you can start it swinging a little at a time and gradually come back with added force, until finally you can close in a burst of dramatic oratory, with the jury inflamed to white rage against the other side. But if you try to talk to a jury for as much as fifteen minutes, and harp continually upon one line, you will find that the jurors have quit listening to you before you finish."

A look of dawning hope came over the young man's face.

"Then you're going to try and stampede the jury this afternoon?" he asked.

"Yes," said Perry Mason, "this afternoon I'm going to bust that case wide open. By not objecting, by not cross-examining, except upon minor points, I am speeding the case up. Claude Drumm, in spite of himself, finds his case moving so rapidly that it's getting out of hand. The horror sensation that he had expected to be doled out at varying intervals, over a period of three or four days, has all been dumped into the lap of the jury in two hours. It's too much horror for the jury to stand. They're getting ready to seize on some excuse to furnish an emotional relief.

"Claude Drumm expected to fight his way doggedly toward a goal. Instead of that, he finds that there's no resistance whatever. He's galloping down the field with such unexpected speed that his information can't keep up. He's busting his own case wide open."

"And you're going to do something this afternoon?" asked Frank Everly. "You're going to try something of your own?"

"This afternoon," said Perry Mason, his face set in firm lines, his eyes staring fixedly ahead, "I am going to try and get a verdict of not guilty."

He pinched out the cigarette, scraped back his chair.

"Come on, young man," he said, "let's go."

CHAPTER XXI

TRUE to Perry Mason's predictions, Claude Drumm introduced the clerk at the sporting goods store, who had been brought from Santa Barbara. The clerk identified the murder weapon as one that had been sold to the defendant on the 29th day of September of the preceding year. He showed the sale on the register of firearms; showed the signature of Bessie Forbes.

Triumphantly, Claude Drumm made a gesture toward Perry Mason.

"You," he declaimed, "may cross-examine the witness."

"No questions," drawled Perry Mason.

Claude Drumm frowned as the witness left the stand, then turned toward the courtroom and said, dramatically. "Call Thelma Benton."

Thelma Benton gave her testimony in a low, resonant voice. In response to questions by Claude Drumm she sketched rapidly the human drama in the life of the dead man. She told of his life in Santa Barbara; of the infatuation with Paula Cartright; of the elopement; of the purchase of the house on Milpas Drive; of the happiness of Forbes and his companion, in their illicit romance; then the mysterious tenant of the adjoining house; the continued inspection through binoculars; the sudden realization that this neighbor was none other than the wronged

188

husband; the abrupt departure of Paula Cartright, and then of the murder.

"Cross-examine," declaimed Claude Drumm triumphantly.

Perry Mason got slowly to his feet.

"Your Honor," he said, "it will be readily apparent that this witness may, perhaps, be a witness whose testimony is of greatest importance. I understand there will be the usual five or ten minutes recess at approximately three-thirty o'clock. It is now three-ten, and I am perfectly willing to commence my cross-examination, and have it interrupted by the usual afternoon recess. But, aside from that interruption, I submit that I should be able to cross-examine this witness without interruption during the rest of the afternoon."

Judge Markham raised his eyebrows and glanced at Claude Drumm.

"There is no objection to that, is there, Mr. District Attorney?" he asked.

"None whatever," said Claude Drumm sneeringly. "Cross-examine as long as you want to."

"I don't wish to be misunderstood," said Perry Mason. "I would like very much either to postpone my cross-examination until tomorrow, or to have it understood that it may be completed today."

"Proceed with the cross-examination, Counselor," said Judge Markham, rapping with his gavel. "This Court has no intention of interrupting the cross-examination by adjournment, if that is what you have in mind."

Claude Drumm made an elaborately polite gesture. "You can cross-examine this witness for a year, if you want to," he said.

"That will do!" snapped Judge Markham. "Proceed with the cross-examination, Counselor."

Perry Mason was once more the center of attention. His intimation that the cross-examination was to be of the greatest importance swung the attention of every one in the courtroom to him. The fact that his previous cross-examinations had been so perfunctory, served to emphasize his cross-examination of this witness.

"When you left Santa Barbara with Mr. Forbes and Mrs. Cartright," he said, "did Mrs. Cartright know of your capacity?"

"I don't know."

"You don't know what Mr. Forbes told her?"

"Naturally not."

"You had previously been the secretary of Mr. Forbes?"

"Yes."

"Had you," asked Perry Mason, "been more than a secretary?"

Claude Drumm was on his feet with a vigorous and vehement objection. Judge Markham promptly sustained the objection.

"It goes to show motive, Your Honor," said Perry Mason.

"The witness has as yet given no testimony which would make any *such* motive of the slightest importance," snapped the Court. "The ruling has been made, Counselor. You will proceed with the cross-examination and avoid such questions in the future."

"Very well," said Perry Mason.

"When you left Santa Barbara with Clinton Forbes and Paula Cartright, you were traveling by automobile, Mrs. Benton?"

"Yes."

"And in that automobile was a police dog?"

"Yes."

"A police dog named Prince?"

"Yes."

"The dog that was killed at the time of the murder?"

"Yes," said Thelma Benton with sudden vehemence. "He gave his life trying to defend his master against the attack of a cowardly assassin!"

Perry Mason nodded slowly. "And that was the dog that came with you in the automobile?"

"Yes."

"That dog was devoted to Paula Cartright?"

"Yes, he was quite friendly with her at the time we left Santa Barbara, and he became very much attached to her."

"And that dog previously had been in the household of Mr. and Mrs. Forbes?"

"That is correct."

"You had seen the dog there?"

"Yes."

"And that dog was also attached to Mrs. Forbes?"

"Naturally."

"The dog also became attached to you?"

"Yes, it was an animal with an affectionate disposition."

"Yes," said Perry Mason, "I can understand that. And the dog howled almost continuously during the night of the fifteenth of October of the present year?"

"It did not."

"Did you hear the dog howl?"

"I did not."

"Isn't it a fact, Mrs. Benton, that the dog left the house, stood near the garage addition which was under construction, and howled dismally?"

"He did not."

"Now," said Perry Mason, abruptly changing the subject, "you have identified the letter which Mrs. Cartright left for Mr. Forbes when she decided to rejoin her husband?"

"Yes."

"She had been confined to her room with influenza?"

"Yes."

"And was recuperating?"

"Yes."

"And she abruptly summoned a taxicab when Mr. Forbes was absent?"

"When Mr. Forbes," said the witness, with icy acidity,

"had been decoyed from the house by a false complaint which had been filed against him with a district attorney, by yourself and Arthur Cartright, the woman rejoined Mr. Cartright. She did it surreptitiously."

"You mean," said Perry Mason, "that she ran away with her own husband."

"She deserted Mr. Forbes, with whom she had been living for a year," said the witness.

"And she left this letter behind?"

"Yes."

"You recognize that letter as being in the handwriting of Mrs. Cartright?"

"I do."

"Were you familiar with the handwriting of Mrs. Cartright before she left Santa Barbara?"

"Yes."

"Now," said Perry Mason, producing a piece of paper, "I show you a paper which purports to be in the handwriting of Mrs. Cartright, and ask you if that handwriting is the same as that on the letter?"

"No," said the witness slowly, "it is not." She bit her lip for a moment, then added suddenly, "Mrs. Cartright, I think, made a conscious attempt to change her handwriting after she left Santa Barbara. She was trying to keep her real identity from being discovered by anyone with whom she might come in contact."

"I see," said Perry Mason. "Now I show you a sheet of paper which purports to contain handwriting by Bessie Forbes, the defendant in this action. That is not the same handwriting as is contained in this letter that Mrs. Cartright left behind her, is it?"

"Certainly not."

"And," said Perry Mason, "may I ask that you write something on a sheet of paper, so that your handwriting may be compared?"

The witness hesitated.

"This is highly irregular, Your Honor," said Claude Drumm, getting to his feet.

Perry Mason shook his head.

"The witness," he said, "has testified as to the handwriting of Mrs. Cartright. I have the right to cross-examine her, by showing her other handwritings, and ask her opinion as to the identity of those handwritings, compared with the writing in the note."

"I think you are right," said Judge Markham. "The objection will be overruled."

Thelma Benton took a sheet of paper, wrote swift lines upon it.

Perry Mason examined the writing and nodded.

"I think we will both concede," he said, "that that is entirely different from the handwriting which appears on the letter which Mrs. Cartright left behind."

"Naturally," said the witness in a tone of cool sarcasm.

Judge Markham fidgeted uneasily.

"It has approached the hour of the usual afternoon recess," he said. "I believe you stated, Counselor, that you had no objection to an interruption of the cross-examination for the usual afternoon recess?"

"None whatever, Your Honor."

"Very well, the Court will take a recess for ten minutes. The jury will remember the admonition of the Court, not to converse about the case or permit it to be discussed in your presence."

The judge arose from his chair, flashed Perry Mason a curiously speculative gaze, then walked into chambers.

Perry Mason looked at his watch and frowned.

"Go over to the window, Frank," he said to Frank Everly, "and see if you can notice any unusual activity on the part of the newsboys at the corner."

The clerk walked to the window of the courtroom, looked down on the street.

Perry Mason, ignoring the concentrated gaze of the curious spectators, slumped down in his chair and bowed his head in thought. His strong, capable fingers made little drumming motions on the arm of the chair.

Frank Everly turned from the window, came running back toward the counsel table.

"There's a lot of excitement down there," he said. "There's been a truck distributing papers. It looks like an extra. The boys are calling them."

Perry Mason looked at the clock and smiled.

"Go on down and pick up a couple of the newspapers," he said.

He turned his head and nodded to Bessie Forbes.

"I'm sorry, Mrs. Forbes," he said, "that you've had such an ordeal, but I don't think it will be long now."

She looked at him with puzzled eyes.

"Frankly," she said, "the talk that I overheard this noon was that the case was going very badly against me."

The deputy sheriff who had her in charge moved slightly forward in order to be at her side. Claude Drumm, who had been smoking a cigarette in the corridor, came stalking back into the courtroom, his importance entirely reestablished in his own mind. He strode with well-tailored efficiency, a dignified superiority toward the criminal attorney who must needs make his living from the trial of cases, rather than bask in the dignity of a monthly salary check, issued with the clock-like regularity with which government officials expend the money of taxpayers.

Frank Everly came bursting into the courtroom with two newspapers, his eyes wide, his lips sagging open.

"They've found the bodies!" he shouted, and rushed toward Perry Mason.

Perry Mason picked up one of the newspapers and held it so that the startled eyes of Claude Drumm could see the headlines.

"Millionaire's Mansion Is Murder Farm," screamed in glaring headlines across the entire front of the page. Lower, and in slightly smaller type, appeared the words:

"BODIES OF CARTRIGHT AND WIFE DISCOVERED UNDER FLOOR OF FORBES' GARAGE."

Claude Drumm sat bolt erect, stared with bulging eyes. A bailiff rushed into the courtroom carrying a newspaper, and went on a half run into the judge's chambers. A spectator entered the courtroom with an open newspaper, babbling excitedly. Within a matter of seconds, he was the center of a circle that listened with bated breath.

Claude Drumm abruptly reached forward.

"May I see that newspaper?" he snapped.

"Delighted," said Perry Mason, and handed him the second newspaper.

Thelma Benton walked swiftly over to Claude Drumm.

"I've got to see you a moment," she said.

Perry Mason glanced through the account in the newspaper, passed it over to Frank Everly.

"Go ahead and read it, Frank," he said. "Looks like *The Chronicle* had a scoop."

"But why didn't the officers know about it?"

"They probably used friendly deputies and kept it sewed up until they could get a paper on the street. If it had hit the general office at headquarters, every newspaper in the city would have been onto it."

Perry Mason looked at the clock, then arose, stretched, yawned, and sauntered into the chambers of Judge Markham.

The judge sat at his table reading the newspaper account, with eyes that held an expression of puzzled bewilderment.

"I don't like to bother you, Judge," said Perry Mason, "but I notice that the time allotted for the recess is up. I am very anxious to conclude my examination of this witness prior to the evening adjournment. In fact, I think that it may well be possible that we can get the case disposed of today."

Judge Markham looked up at Perry Mason, his eyes glinting shrewdly.

"I am wondering," he said, "as to the purpose . . ." His voice trailed into silence.

"Yes?" said Perry Mason.

"Yes," said Judge Markham drily.

"Just what were you wondering, Judge?" said Perry Mason.

Judge Markham frowned.

"I don't know as I should discuss it," he said, "but I am wondering at the peculiar nature of the request you made that you be allowed to complete your cross-examination of the witness today."

Perry Mason shrugged his shoulders and said nothing.

"Either," Judge Markham said, "you are the most remarkably lucky man practicing at the bar, or else the most shrewdly adroit; I can't tell which."

Perry Mason did not answer the question directly, but said instead, "I have always figured that a lawsuit was like an iceberg—only a fraction of it was visible to the naked eye; the balance of it is beneath the surface."

Judge Markham got to his feet.

"Well, Counselor," he said, "be that as it may, you are entitled to go on with the case."

Perry Mason walked back to the courtroom. Almost immediately Judge Markham entered from his chambers. The bailiff pounded frantically for order, and pounded for several seconds before his admonitions were heeded. The courtroom was in a seething uproar of buzzing conversation, excited comments, scurrying motion.

Order, at length, was restored. The jurors took their seats. Perry Mason slumped in his chair, apparently utterly unmoved by the startling events of the last few minutes.

"Thelma Benton was on the stand for further cross-examination," said Judge Markham.

Claude Drumm got to his feet.

"Your Honor," he said, "a most startling and unexpected development has taken place. In view of the circumstances, I know that Your Honor will not require me to mention the nature of that development, at least in the presence of the jury. But I feel that as an officer of the state, as a deputy prosecutor who is familiar with the facts of this case, my presence is urgently required elsewhere, and I request an adjournment of this case until tomorrow morning."

Judge Markham looked over his glasses at Perry Mason.

"Any objections, Counselor?" he asked.

"Yes," said Perry Mason, getting to his feet. "The rights of the defendant demand that the cross-examination of this witness be concluded at this session of the court. I mentioned this matter before I started the cross-examination, and that was the specific understanding which I had with counsel."

"That is correct," said Judge Markham. "The request for a continuance will be denied."

"But," shouted Claude Drumm, "Your Honor must understand. . . ."

"That will do, Counselor," said Judge Markham. "The motion for a continuance has been denied. Proceed, Mr. Mason."

Perry Mason looked at Thelma Benton for a moment with a long, steady stare of accusation.

She lowered her eyes and fidgeted on the witness stand. Her face was as white as the wall in back of her.

"Now," said Perry Mason slowly, "as I understand your testimony, Paula Cartright left the residence on Milpas Drive in a taxicab on the morning of October 17th."

"That is correct," she said.

"You saw her leave?"

"Yes," she said in a low voice.

"Do I understand," said Perry Mason, raising his voice, "that you saw Paula Cartright alive on the morning of October 17th of this year?"

The witness bit her lip, hesitated.

"Let the records show," said Perry Mason urbanely, "that the witness hesitates."

Claude Drumm jumped to his feet.

"That," he said, "is manifestly unfair, and I object to the question, as argumentative; as already asked and answered; as not being proper cross-examination."

"The objection is overruled," said Judge Markham. "The record will show that the witness hesitates appreciably in answering."

Thelma Benton looked up. Her eyes were dark with panic.

"I can't say that I saw her personally," she said. "I heard steps going down the stairs from her room. I saw a taxicab drawn up in front of the place, and I saw a woman getting into the taxicab, then the cab drove away. I took it for granted that the woman was Mrs. Cartright."

"Then you didn't see her?" pressed Perry Mason.

"No," she said in a low voice, "I didn't see her."

"Now," said Perry Mason, "you have identified this letter as being in the handwriting of Mrs. Cartright."

"Yes, sir."

Perry Mason produced the photostatic copy of the telegram which had been sent from Midwick.

"And," he said, "will you identify the photostatic copy of this telegram as also being in the handwriting of Paula Cartright?"

The witness looked at the telegram, hesitated, bit her lip.

"They're the same handwriting, are they not?" asked Perry Mason—"those two documents?"

When she answered, her voice was so low as to be almost inaudible.

"Yes," she said, "I guess they're in the same handwriting."

"Don't you know?" said Perry Mason. "You unhesitatingly identified the letter as being in the handwriting of Paula Cartright. How about this telegram? Is that, or is that not, in the handwriting of Paula Cartright?"

"Yes," said the witness in an almost inaudible voice, "it is Mrs. Cartright's handwriting."

"So," said Perry Mason, "Mrs. Cartright sent this telegram from Midwick on the morning of October 17th?"

"I guess so," said the witness in a low voice.

Judge Markham pounded with his gavel.

"Mrs. Benton," he said, "you've got to speak up so the jury can understand you. Speak more loudly, please."

She raised her head, stared at the judge, and swayed slightly.

Claude Drumm was on his feet.

"Your Honor," he said, "it now appears that the witness is ill. I again ask for a continuance, out of justice to this witness, who has doubtless sustained a very great shock."

Judge Markham slowly shook his head.

"I think the cross-examination should continue," he said.

"If," said Claude Drumm in pleading desperation, "this case can be continued until tomorrow, there is some chance it might be dismissed."

Perry Mason whirled about and stood with his feet planted firmly on the floor, spread slightly apart; his head thrust forward, his manner belligerent; his voice raised until it seemed to echo in the rafters of the courtroom.

"If the Court please," he thundered, "that is exactly the situation I wish to avoid. A public accusation has been made against the defendant in this case, and the defendant is entitled to an acquittal at the hands of a jury. A dismissal by the prosecution would still leave her with a blot upon her name."

Judge Markham's voice sounded low and even-toned, compared with the vehement eloquence of Perry Mason.

"The motion is once more denied," he said. "The case will continue."

"Now," said Perry Mason, "will you kindly explain

how Paula Cartright could write a letter and a telegram on the morning of October 17th of this year, when you know, of your own knowledge, that Paula Cartright was murdered on the evening of October 16th?"

Claude Drumm was on his feet.

"That," he said, "is objected to as argumentative, calling for a conclusion of the witness, not proper cross-examination and assuming a fact not in evidence."

Judge Markham paused for a moment, stared at the white, drawn face of the witness.

"I am going to sustain the objection," he said.

Perry Mason reached for the letter which had been identified as being in the handwriting of Mrs. Cartright, placed it on the table in front of the witness, and pounded it with his fist.

"Didn't you write that letter?" he asked of the witness.

"No!" she flared.

"Isn't it your handwriting?"

"You know that it is not," she said. "The handwriting doesn't resemble mine in the least."

"On the 17th day of October," said Perry Mason, "your right hand was in a bandage, was it not?"

"Yes."

"You had been bitten by a dog."

"Yes. Prince had been poisoned, and when I tried to give him an emetic he accidentally bit my hand."

"Yes," said Perry Mason. "But the fact remains that your right hand was bandaged on the 17th day of October of this year, and remained bandaged for several days thereafter, isn't that right?"

"Yes."

"And you couldn't hold a pen in that hand?"

There was a moment of silence, then the witness said suddenly: "Yes. And that goes to show how false your accusation is that I wrote that letter or that telegram. My hand was crippled so that I couldn't possibly have held a pen in it."

"Were you," snapped Perry Mason, "in Midwick on the 17th day of October of this year?"

The witness hesitated.

"Didn't you," went on Perry Mason without waiting for an answer, "charter an airplane and fly to Midwick on the 17th day of October of this year?"

"Yes," said the witness, "I thought I might find Mrs. Cartright in Midwick, and I went there by plane."

"And didn't you file this telegram at the telegraph office in Midwick while you were there?" asked Perry Mason.

"No," she said, "I have told you that I couldn't have written that telegram."

"Very well," said Perry Mason, "let's go back a moment to this mangled hand of yours. It was so badly mangled you couldn't possibly hold a pen in your right hand?"

"Yes."

"And that was on the 17th day of October of this year?"

"Yes."

"Also on the 18th day of October?"

"Yes."

"Also on the 19th?"

"Yes."

"Very well," said Perry Mason, "isn't it a fact that you kept a diary over the period I have mentioned?"

"Yes," she said swiftly, before she thought, then suddenly caught her breath, bit her lip and said, "No."

"Which is it," said Perry Mason, "yes or no?"

"No," she said.

Perry Mason whipped a torn sheet of paper from his pocket.

"As a matter of fact," he said, "isn't that a sheet of paper which came from a diary which you kept on or about that date—to wit, the 18th of October of this year?"

The witness stared at the torn piece of paper, said nothing.

"And isn't it," said Perry Mason, "a fact that you are ambidextrous; that you were keeping the diary during that time, and that you made entries in it with a pen that was held in your left hand? Isn't it a fact that you have always been able to write with your left hand, and that you do so whenever you wish to disguise your writing? Isn't it a fact that you have in your possession such a diary, from which this is a torn leaf, and that the handwriting on this torn leaf is exactly identical with the handwriting shown on the letter purported to have been written by Paula Cartright, and on the telegram purported to have been filed by her?"

The witness rose to her feet, looked at Judge Markham with glassy eyes, stared at the jury, then parted her white lips and screamed.

Bedlam broke loose in the courtroom. Bailiffs pounded for order. Deputies ran toward the witness.

Claude Drumm was on his feet, frantically shouting a motion for adjournment which was lost in the turmoil of noise.

Perry Mason walked back to the counsel table and sat down.

Deputies reached the side of Thelma Benton. They took her elbows and started to pilot her from the witness stand. She abruptly pitched forward in a dead faint.

The voice of Claude Drumm made itself audible above the confused roar of the courtroom.

"Your Honor," he shouted, "in the name of common decency, in the name of humanity, I demand a continuation of this case, in order to enable this witness to regain some measure of composure and health, before there is any further cross-examination. It is apparent, regardless of the cause, that she is a very sick woman. To continue with such a merciless cross-examination at this time is lacking in decency and humanity!"

Judge Markham slitted his eyes in thought, glanced over at Perry Mason.

Perry Mason's voice was low and calm, and the hubbub in the courtroom quieted so that spectators might hear him.

"May I ask counsel if that is the only reason he is asking for a continuance?" said Perry Mason.

"Certainly," said Claude Drumm.

"May I also ask counsel," said Perry Mason, "in view of the request for a continuance, if he has any other witnesses, or if this is his last witness?"

"This," said Claude Drumm, "is my last witness. I grant counsel the right to cross-examine her. The district attorney's office joins with counsel in a desire to find out the true facts of this case.

"But I cannot consent to the continuation of a cross-examination of a woman who is manifestly suffering from such a terrific nerve strain."

"I think, Counselor," said Judge Markham, "that the motion at this time is well taken, at least for a short continuance."

Perry Mason's smile was urbane.

"Your Honor," he said, "the motion for a continuance is no longer necessary. It gives me pleasure to announce that in view of the mental state of the witness, and my desire to complete the case, I am finished with my cross-examination."

He sat down.

Claude Drumm stood by his chair at the counsel table, staring incredulously at Perry Mason.

"You're finished?" he asked.

"Yes," said Perry Mason.

"Under those circumstances," said Claude Drumm, "I am taken by surprise, Your Honor, and I would like to have the case continued until tomorrow morning."

"For what reason?" asked Judge Markham.

"Simply in order to get my mind clear upon certain

facts, and to ascertain what course I desire to take," said Claude Drumm.

"But," pointed out Judge Markham, "in response to a question by counsel, you have stated that this was your last witness."

"Very well," said Claude Drumm suddenly. "I rest. Let counsel go ahead with his defense."

Perry Mason bowed to the court and to the jury.

"The defendant," he said, "also rests."

"What?" shouted Claude Drumm. "You are putting on no evidence whatever?"

"The defendant," said Perry Mason with dignity, "rests."

The voice of Judge Markham was calm and judicial.

"Do you gentlemen desire to argue the case?" he asked.

"Yes," said Perry Mason, "I would like to argue the case."

"And you, Counselor?" the judge asked of Claude Drumm.

"Your Honor, I cannot argue this case at the present time. It will require some preparation. Once more I ask for an adjournment. . . ."

"Once more," he said, in a tone of finality, "the request is denied. I feel that the rights of the defendant in this case are entitled to consideration at the hands of the Court. Go ahead and argue, Mr. Drumm."

Claude Drumm got to his feet.

"Your Honor," he said, "I think I shall ask the Court for a dismissal of this case."

The court nodded. "Very well," he said, "if . . ."

Perry Mason was on his feet.

"Your Honor," he said, "I object to the motion. I believe that I have previously stated my position in regard to it. The defendant in this case is entitled to have her name cleared. A dismissal of the case would not do that."

Judge Markham's eyes suddenly narrowed. He looked

at Perry Mason with the wary watchfulness of a cat regarding a mouse hole.

"Do I understand, Counselor, that you object to a dismissal of this case by the prosecution?"

"I do."

"Very well," said Judge Markham, "we will let the jury take the case. The deputy district attorney will proceed with the argument."

Claude Drumm got to his feet, walked toward the jury box.

"Gentlemen of the jury," he said, "there has been a most unexpected development in this case. I do not know what course I should have taken, had the case been continued so that I could give a complete consideration to the facts. However, as the facts now stand, the defendant in this case is shown to have been present at the house where the murder was committed, at the time the murder was committed. She is shown to have had a motive strong enough to impel her to murder the decedent. The gun with which the killing was done was a gun which she had purchased. Under the circumstances, I feel that she should not be acquitted. I am frank to state I do not feel that the state should ask for the death penalty. I am frank to state that I am somewhat confused by the sudden turn of events, but I feel that these matters should be considered by you. Gentlemen, I have nothing further to say."

In savage dignity Claude Drumm strode back to the counsel table and resumed his seat.

Perry Mason approached the jurors, stared at them quizzically for a few moments.

"Gentlemen," he said, "a fortunate break on the part of the main witness for the prosecution has saved you the possibility of working an irreparable wrong upon an innocent woman.

"The evidence in this case is purely circumstantial. From the circumstances of the case, the prosecution is entitled to make any deductions it desires; also, the defense is entitled to make any deductions it desires.

"Let me, therefore, take the circumstances of this case and outline to you first, the impossibility of the crime having been committed by the defendant, and, second, the possibility that it was committed by some other person.

"In the first place, the evidence shows that the person who murdered Clinton Forbes entered the house either with a passkey or with a key which was rightfully in the possession of such person. The evidence shows that that person went to the room where Forbes was engaged in shaving. The evidence shows that Forbes strode out of his bedroom into the library to see who the intruder was; that he then became alarmed, ran back to the bathroom, and liberated the police dog which had been chained in the bathroom. It is apparent that when he heard some one in the library, Forbes mopped the lather from his face with a towel as he walked out to the library. After he beheld the intruder, he ran back to the bathroom and unchained the dog. As he did so, he used both hands to unchain the dog, and dropped the towel containing the lather which had been wiped from his face. This towel was dropped near the edge of the bathtub, in exactly the position where it would have been dropped, logically and naturally, under the circumstances. The dog sprang toward the intruder with bared teeth, and as counsel for the prosecution has so aptly remarked, and as witnesses for the prosecution have so truthfully testified, endeavored to save the life of his master. The assassin shot the dog at close quarters. The powder burns are on the fur of the dog. That shows that the dog was actually attacking the murderer when the shots were fired.

"After those shots were fired, the intruder grappled with Clinton Forbes. It will never be known whether the intruder came to meet Clinton Forbes, or whether Forbes rushed to meet the intruder, but the shots which killed Forbes were fired at close range.

"Gentlemen, it is the contention of the prosecution that those shots were fired by the defendant in this case.

"There is, gentlemen, one unanswerable objection to such a theory. That is, that if the intruder had been the defendant in this case, the police dog would not have rushed upon the defendant; nor would it have been necessary for the defendant to have shot the dog. The dog knew the defendant and loved her. The dog would never have charged upon the defendant under those circumstances, but would rather have given vent to joyous barks of canine gratification that the two persons whom it loved had been reunited.

"That, gentlemen, disposes of the case of the prosecution.

"Under the law relating to circumstantial evidence, it is necessary that before a conviction can be had at the hands of a jury, the jurors must be convinced that the circumstances can be explained upon no reasonable hypothesis, other than the guilt of the defendant.

"Now, let me point out the significant circumstances which indicate that the murder was committed by some other person:

"There is evidence in this case that Arthur Cartright complained of a dog howling on the premises of Clinton Forbes, on the night of October 15th. The dog howled continuously during the night, the howls being from the back of the house and in the neighborhood of the addition to the garage which was being duly constructed.

"Gentlemen, let us suppose that there had been an altercation between Paula Cartright and Clinton Forbes. Let us suppose that Clinton Forbes. during that altercation, had murdered Paula Cartright Let us suppose that he and Thelma Benton, together, had scooped out a shallow grave in the soil where the cement floor of the new garage building was to be poured. And we might even suppose, in view of the terms of the note which Thelma Benton subsequently wrote, as purporting to come from the pen of Paula Cartright, then the quarrel resulted from the discovery of an intimacy between Forbes and Thelma Benton by Paula Cartright.

"Mrs. Cartright had given up her social position, her right to be considered a respectable member of society, in order to run away with Clinton Forbes, where she lived with him under such circumstances that she was barred from all friendships of her past life; could form no new friendships; was a woman continually haunted by the fear of discovery. And then she found that the sacrifice she had made was for nothing; that the love she thought she had gained by such a sacrifice was, in reality, a hollow mockery, and that Clinton Forbes was no more true to her than he had been true to the wife whom he had deserted in Santa Barbara.

"Paula Cartright quarreled bitterly and her lips were sealed forever by the two assassins who secretly buried her body. The Chinese cook was asleep. Only the stars of the night and the guilty consciences of the murderous pair who scooped out the shallow grave knew what was going on. But there was one other who knew. That was a faithful police dog. He smelled the cold corpse. He knew that it was interred in a shallow grave and he watched by that grave and howled.

"Arthur Cartright had been watching the house. He didn't realize the significance of the steady howling of the dog, but it did prey upon his overwrought nerves. He took steps to see that the dog did not howl any more, thinking at the time he instituted such steps that the howling of the dog was nothing more than a vagary of the canine mind. But at some time during the next night, the frightful significance of those howls dawned upon him. The possibility crashed home, that the dog was mourning the passing of one whom the dog held dear. His mind filled with suspicion, Arthur Cartright set out to investigate.

"Clinton Forbes and his pseudo-housekeeper had embarked upon a career of murder. They found themselves confronted with an accusation of the crime. A man who was almost as one bereft of reason demanded that he be confronted with Paula Cartright, in order that he might see for himself that she was alive and well.

"Gentlemen," said Perry Mason, lowering his voice impressively, "there was only one thing which the conspirators could do to preserve their secret. There was one more ghastly step which they had to take in order to put the seal of silence upon the lips of the man who was mouthing accusations which they knew would soon be made to the authorities, and would soon result in an investigation. They fell upon him and murdered him, as they had murdered his wife, and they buried his body beside hers, knowing that on the next day, the cement workers would pour cement over the place where the shallow graves were located, forever sealing off the ghastly evidence of the dastardly crime.

"The guilty pair were then confronted with the necessity of explaining the simultaneous absence of both Arthur Cartright and his wife. There was only one way they could do it, and that was by making it appear that husband and wife had become reunited and had run away together. Thelma Benton was ambidextrous. This fact was known to Clinton Forbes. He also knew that it was extremely unlikely any one would have any specimen of the genuine handwriting of Paula Cartright. She was a woman estranged from the world; one who had burnt her bridges behind her. She had no friends to whom she cared to write. There was no one to come forward with a specimen of the woman's handwriting. So the letter was forged. The name was signed, the bridges were burnt once more, and once more the guilty pair proceeded upon their career of deception.

"Gentlemen, I need not mention to you the inevitable result of such a combination of wickedness, founded upon crime, nurtured in deception, and culminating in murder. There were two conspirators, each of whom knew that the other had the power to send the long arm of the law swooping down in righteous reprisal. Thelma Benton was the first to act. She left the house at six o'clock and repaired to a rendezvous with a male friend. What she said to him, we need not ask. We are only concerned with what happened. And, mind you, I am making no case against Thelma Benton and her accomplice, but am only pointing out to you what *might* have happened, as a reasonable hypothesis upon which the evidence can be explained. Thelma Benton and her accomplice returned to the house. They entered, by using the key of the pseudo-housekeeper. Upon guilty feet, the pair stalked their living prey, as though he had been a beast of the jungle. But the sensitive ears of the dog heard and interpreted that which was happening. Alarmed by the barking of the dog, Clinton Forbes stepped out of the bathroom. He saw his housekeeper standing there, and wiped the lather from his face as he started to talk to her. Then he saw the man who was with her, and knew the purpose of her visit. In a panic, he rushed to the bathroom and liberated the dog. The dog sprang at the masculine intruder, and the man shot. The dog fell lifeless to the floor. Forbes struggled with the woman and then there were two more shots fired at close range, and then—silence."

Perry Mason came to an abrupt halt. He stared seriously, solemnly at the jury. In a voice that was so low it could hardly be heard, he said, "Gentlemen, that is all."

He turned and walked back to his seat.

Claude Drumm stared uncertainly at the jury, at the judge, at the hostile faces of those in the courtroom, then shrugged his shoulders.

"No argument," he said.

CHAPTER XXII

IT WAS more than two hours after the verdict had been returned, when Perry Mason entered his office. It was long since dark, but Della Street was waiting for him, her eyes starry. Paul Drake was also in the office, lounging on the edge of a desk, his droll features twisted in placid humor while a cigarette dangled listlessly from the corner of his mouth.

Perry Mason was leading a police dog on a leash.

The pair stared at the police dog, then at Mason.

"By George," said Paul Drake, "you certainly have a genius for the dramatic and spectacular. Now that you have used a dog in order to get an acquittal, you're going to adopt a police dog and lead him around with you. It will serve to keep every one familiar with your dramatic triumph."

"Not necessarily," said Perry Mason. "Let me put the dog in the closet here. He's nervous, and I think it would be better for him to go in there."

He led the dog to the closet in his private office, unleashed the animal, bedded him down on the floor, reassured him with low, crooning conversation, and then closed, but did not latch, the door. He turned to receive the handshake of Paul Drake, and then Della Street's arms were about his neck, crushing him down to her as she danced in an ecstasy of glee.

"Oh," she said, "it was so wonderful! I read your argument in the paper. They got out an extra in which they set forth your arguments verbatim. It was simply wonderful!"

"The newspapers," said Paul Drake, "are calling you the Master of Courtroom Drama."

"Just a lucky break," said Perry Mason modestly.

"Lucky nothing," Paul Drake said. "That thing was carefully planned. You had about six strings to your bow. If you had been forced to do it, you could have used the evidence of the Chinese cook to show that the dog did howl. If you had been forced to, you could have put Mae Sibley on the stand and made the whole case a joke. You could have done any one of a dozen things."

Della Street said excitedly, "As soon as I read your argument, I knew the chain of reasoning by which you had realized where the bodies were . . ."

Abruptly she glanced at Paul Drake and broke off.

"But," said Drake, "there are two or three things about your argument that don't hang together. In the first place, if Thelma Benton had returned to the house with this chap, Carl Trask, and they had murdered Forbes, why wouldn't Wheeler and Doake have seen them drive up?"

"Wheeler and Doake weren't witnesses," said Perry Mason.

"I know that," said the detective. "You saw to that by seeing to it that the district attorney didn't know you had shadows watching the house. If he had known all that those two fellows knew, he would have moved heaven and earth to get them."

"Was it fair to let them get out of the jurisdiction of the court?" asked Della Street dubiously.

Perry Mason stood with his legs wide apart, his shoulders squared, his jaw thrust forward.

"Listen, you two," he said, "I've told you before, and I'm telling you again, that I'm not a judge and I'm not a jury. I'm a lawyer. The district attorney does everything he can to build up a strong case against the defendant. It's up to the lawyer for the defendant to do everything he can to break down the case for the district attorney. Look at that taxicab driver, for instance. You know, and I know, that that taxicab driver couldn't have identified the woman who left that handkerchief in his taxicab; not in a million years. He knew that she used a peculiar type of perfume, and he knew, generally, how she was dressed. He knew something about her build, and that was all he knew. We demonstrated that effectively by having Mae Sibley go to him and show just how fallible a thing his identification was. Yet, the district attorney, with all of the machinery of the state at his back, carried on a subtle campaign of suggestion by which he actually convinced

212

the taxi driver, not only that he could positively identify the woman, but that there was no question but what that woman was the defendant in the action.

"That is the sort of tactics we had to meet in this case. That is the sort of tactics a lawyer for the defense always has to meet. I'm telling you that he's not a judge and he's not a jury; he's merely a partisan, a representative hired by the defendant, with the sanction of the state, whose solemn duty it is to present the case of the defendant in its strongest light.

"That's my creed and that's what I try to do."

"Well," said Drake, "you skated on pretty thin ice in this case, but you certainly got away with it. You're entitled to congratulations. The newspapers are giving you millions of dollars worth of advertisement. You're considered a legal wizard, and, by God, you are!"

He extended his hand, and Mason took it.

"Well," said Drake, "I'll be down in the office for a while, if there's anything else you want to check up on. I suppose you're tired and want to get home and get some rest."

"Things *have* been coming pretty fast," said Perry Mason, "but I like the excitement."

Drake left the office.

Della Street looked at him with her eyes wide and starry.

"Oh," she said, "I'm so glad. So glad that you got her off. It was wonderful!"

She stared at him for a moment with her lips quivering with words that she could not express, then suddenly flung her arms wide apart, and embraced him once more.

There was the sound of an apologetic cough from the doorway.

Della Street flung back and stared.

Bessie Forbes stood in the doorway.

"Pardon me," she said, "if I intrude. I was liberated

and I came at once to your office as soon as I could get my things together."

"That's all right," said Perry Mason, "we're glad . . ."

There was a wild sound of scrambling motion. The door of the closet slammed open. The police dog catapulted out into the room, with claws scratching and scraping futilely on the hardwood floors. He hit the carpet and launched into speed, dashing directly toward the startled form of Bessie Forbes.

The dog leapt up at her, gave joyous howls. His tongue licked at her face, and she gave a glad cry, stooped and flung her arms about the massive shoulders of the huge police dog.

"Prince!" she said. "Prince!"

"I beg your pardon," said Perry Mason, "but his name is not Prince. Prince is dead."

The woman stared at him with startled, incredulous eyes.

"Down, Prince," she said.

The dog dropped to the floor, where he lay, regarding her with eyes that were limpid with emotion, a tail that thumped ecstatically.

"Where did you get him?" she asked.

"I," said Perry Mason, "could figure out just why it was that the dog howled on the night of October 15th. I couldn't understand why the dog didn't howl on the night of October 16th, if he were still alive. I also could not understand how it happened that a dog that had been living in the house with Thelma Benton for more than a year, could suddenly have gone savage and attacked her so as to badly mangle her right hand.

"After the case was over, I made a round of kennels in the neighborhood. I found a kennel where an owner had exchanged a police dog on the night of October 16th for another police dog that was very similar in appearance. I purchased the dog that had been left."

"But," said Bessie Forbes, "what are you going to do with him?"

"I," Perry Mason said, "am going to give him to you. He needs a good home. I suggest that you take him with you, and I would further suggest that you leave town at once."

He brought the dog's leash and handed it to her.

"Let us know where you are," he said, "so that we can keep in touch with you. You're the beneficiary under a will. But you will be approached and interviewed by newspaper men. They will ask you embarrassing questions. It might be well if you were not available."

She stared at him wordlessly for a moment, then suddenly extended her hand.

"Thank you," she said, then turned abruptly.

"Prince," she said, "on my side."

The dog marched from the office, pacing along at her side, matching step for step with his mistress, his plume elevated, waving proudly in the air.

When the door of the outer office closed, Della Street stared at Perry Mason with sudden consternation.

"But," she said, "the only real argument that you had to convince the jury that Bessie Forbes was not the one who did the shooting was that the dog sprang at her. If Clinton Forbes had substituted dogs . . ."

Her voice trailed away into silence.

"I have repeatedly told you," said Perry Mason, "that I am not a judge; nor am I a jury. On the other hand, I have never heard the story of Bessie Forbes; nor has any one else. It may have been that anything she did was done in self-defense. I feel certain that it was. She had to defend herself against a dog and a man. But I acted only as her lawyer."

"But," said Della Street, "they'll get her and try her all over again."

Perry Mason smiled and shook his head.

"Oh, no, they won't," he said. "That's why I wouldn't

let them dismiss the case. A dismissal wouldn't have been a bar to another prosecution. Now she has faced a jury and has been once in jeopardy. She can never be tried again for that offense, as long as she lives, regardless of what other evidence might be uncovered."

"You," said Della Street, staring at him, "are a cross between a saint and a devil."

"All men are," said Perry Mason, unperturbed.

Case after case of
Mystery, Suspense and Intrigue...

ERLE STANLEY GARDNER'S
PERRY MASON MYSTERIES

12